HOMICIDE AT
BLUE HERON LAKE

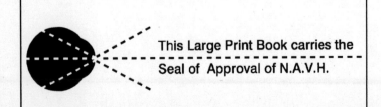
This Large Print Book carries the Seal of Approval of N.A.V.H.

MAINELY MYSTERIES, BOOK ONE

HOMICIDE AT BLUE HERON LAKE

A ROMANCE MYSTERY

SUSAN PAGE DAVIS AND MEGAN ELAINE DAVIS

THORNDIKE PRESS
A part of Gale, Cengage Learning

GALE
CENGAGE Learning™

Detroit • New York • San Francisco • New Haven, Conn • Waterville, Maine • London

GALE
CENGAGE Learning™

LIBRARY OF CONGRESS CATALOGING-IN-PUBLICATION DATA

Davis, Susan Page.
  Homicide at Blue Heron Lake : a romance mystery / by Susan Page Davis and Megan Elaine Davis.
    p. cm. — (Mainely mysteries ; bk. 1) (Thorndike Press large print Christian mystery)
  ISBN-13: 978-1-4104-3303-9 (hardcover)
  ISBN-10: 1-4104-3303-X (hardcover)
  1. Murder—Investigation—Fiction. 2. Maine—Fiction. 3. Large type books. I. Davis, Megan Elaine. II. Title.
PS3604.A976H66 2010
813'.6—dc22   2010036998

Published in 2010 by arrangement with Barbour Publishing, Inc.

Printed in Mexico
1 2 3 4 5 6 7 14 13 12 11 10

For Page — little sister, mother hen, elite friend, partner in crime, and founder of the iced-tea-drinking contest. Long live the Collective Bomb.

Megan

To my brother Gil, who let me use his train set when the girls were all off at camp, helped me learn to ride a bike, and taught me about sonar arrays. Someday I'll come to Mississippi for that sailing lesson.

Susan

1

Emily Gray climbed out of her car and stood still for a moment, taking in the scene. Nothing had changed, and a warm sense of coming home spread through her. In this little town, her happiest memories had been created when her family lived in a log home on the shore of Blue Heron Lake. But some of her worst memories began here, too, and tangled up in both the best and the worst of her past was Nate Holman.

She leaned against her car door, scanning the marina sprawled along the lakeshore. Beside the store she glimpsed the docks, where dozens of watercraft were tied. From canoes and small motorboats, up to a pontoon party boat, a customer could rent whatever vessel he wanted from the Holman family. The sign over the door told her the Baxter, Maine, post office was still tucked into a corner of the emporium.

Breathing almost hurt. How could she

have forgotten the crisp, evergreen-tinged air of northern Maine? Even though it was early June, the cool breeze off the lake made her shiver.

Emily used to tell herself she'd outgrown Baxter. It was too small. An investigative journalist couldn't make a living in a place like this — a tiny community buried in the woods. But now she realized how badly she'd wanted an excuse to come back.

As she pushed open the door, her heart began to race. Was Nate still here or had he fled Baxter the way she had?

She looked around the store. Straight ahead were souvenir T-shirts and small items emblazoned with "Blue Heron Lake" and "Baxter, Maine: the way life should be." Beyond the displays were groceries, casual clothing, housewares, linens, and yes, in the back corner, the post office window. To her left was the nautical area. Kayaks, life jackets, live bait, ropes, cleats, oars, gas cans . . . anything for small boats was available at the Baxter Marina.

As a customer stooped to examine an outboard motor, the clerk reached to a high shelf for a boxed item, his back to Emily. Could it be Mr. Holman? She smiled, anticipating a reunion with Nate's father. As he turned, she caught her breath. It was

8

Nate, not Mr. Holman, who was helping the customer.

Her pulse skyrocketed, and she ducked around the souvenir display. Forcing herself to breathe deeply and evenly, she berated herself.

What is the matter with you, Emily Rachel Gray? He's grown up. What did you expect?

The truth was, she had expected him to be gone — but had longed with an aching hope to see him again.

She heard him and the customer chatting amiably as they walked to the cash register. Emily peeked around the shelf of moose figurines and bags of chocolate-dipped blueberries to watch as he rang up the man's purchase. The customer was Marvin Vigue, she realized, the father of her old classmate, Sarah. The family had a cottage on Grand Cat Island, near the one Emily's family owned.

But her gaze didn't stay long on Marvin. It skipped back to Nate, and Emily's pulse hammered. He was the same . . . only better. His dark hair was a little shorter than he wore it in high school, but it still held a rebellious wave over his forehead. Nate's brown eyes twinkled as he laughed at some inanity of Marvin's and counted out his change. Emily gulped. Nate at twenty-five was a cut above her cherished memories. Maturity enhanced his boyish good looks, and he had a new solidity in his posture and purpose in every movement.

She couldn't help remembering the best/ worst night of her life. That brief moment in Nate's arms . . . Her first kiss . . . She wondered if he remembered.

Breathe, Emily! She hoped no one else would enter the store.

Mr. Vigue collected his package and receipt, said good-bye to Nate, and strode toward the doorway. As he passed Emily, he glanced at her and nodded.

"Hello," she murmured.

He smiled without recognition, and she was glad. The door closed behind him, and she turned with resolution toward the checkout. To her dismay, Nate had advanced half the distance toward her.

"May I help you?" he asked with a smile that held just a hint of puzzlement. He scanned her face and hair, and his gaze came back to her eyes.

"Nate." She stepped toward him and extended her hand.

She could tell the exact moment when he placed her, and his shock was satisfying. He almost gulped for air.

"Em!"

She chuckled. "Yes, Nate. It's me."

He engulfed her hand in both his warm ones. "I . . . can't believe it. After all this time."

"I didn't know if you'd still be here," she said.

"Well, yeah, I'm here just about all the time now, when I'm not out on the lake."

"I'm glad. I mean . . . that we met again. I don't . . ." She stopped in confusion. Something had gone awry in Nate's life. It must have, or he wouldn't be here ringing up spark plugs for Marvin Vigue.

He smiled and shrugged. "It's okay. I just . . . well, when my dad died —"

"Oh, Nate, I'm sorry! I didn't know." Emily touched his sleeve. How awful for her to have bumbled into his sorrow like this.

"No, really, it's all right." He sighed then met her gaze again. "Dad died two years ago. He was sick for a long time, and I had to leave the university after my sophomore year."

She nodded. "I'm sorry. You wanted so much to be a police officer."

"Yeah, well . . ." He looked around at the store. "I guess things haven't changed much since you were here last."

"Not much. New postcards." She nodded at the rack that held the four-for-a-dollar

11

views of the lake.

Nate laughed. "It's so good to see you! What are you doing here?"

"Well, you remember Brian?"

"Your stepfather? How could I forget him?"

Emily winced. "Yes, well . . ." She wished she could have made her explanation without mentioning Brian Gillespie. "He . . . passed away last winter —"

"No. Emily, I'm sorry. I shouldn't have said what I did."

She shook her head, but couldn't meet his eyes. If she did, he would see the painful truth — that she wasn't mourning Brian, either. She managed a smile. "Well, Mom decided to sell the cottage, but she wasn't sure she was up to getting it ready. I had a couple of weeks' vacation coming, so I offered to come up and put it into shape to sell."

Nate let out a long sigh. "They never came up here after they moved to Brunswick."

"No, Mom told me they hadn't been near the place. I guess they rented it out a few times."

He nodded. "Bridget Kaplin handled it, didn't she? Over at Blue Heron Realty."

"That's right," Emily said. "She thinks she can find a buyer fairly quickly."

"Well, sure. Not many island lots come on the market."

Emily glanced toward the post office window. "So, how's your mother?"

"She's fine. We're still living next door."

"She's still the postmistress?"

"Yeah, for fifteen years now."

The door opened and a couple came in, looking about with an air of city people trying to soak up local color.

"Well, you're busy," Emily said. "I was going to ask if you were making a run to Grand Cat today, but it's calm. I can rent a small boat."

"No, let me take you." Nate smiled at the newcomers and called, "I'll be right with you." Turning back to Emily, he lowered his voice. "Can you wait twenty minutes? I've got a couple of orders and some mail for folks out there, and I have to stop at the boys' camp. But I'd really like to take you to your cottage."

She smiled. "Camp Dirigo's still operating?"

"Oh yeah. Bigger and better than ever."

"Go ahead and do what you need to do. I'll take my bags to the dock."

"Great." He grinned at her, and Emily's heart tripped faster. He hadn't changed after all.

"I may need a few groceries, too," she said, looking away and trying to calm her fluttering stomach.

Nate went to help the customers, and she ambled the aisles, stopping at the cooler for a quart of milk and a dozen eggs. She set them on the counter and added a bag of English muffins and a few bananas. Nate was directing the woman to the dairy section. The man shoved his hands in his pockets and drifted toward the kayak display.

Emily left her small order on the counter and went out to her car. An SUV bearing New Jersey license plates was now parked beside it. She took her duffel bag and a large tote bag from the trunk of her car and carried them to the dock. After critically examining the boats nearest the marina's back door, she decided the sleek cabin cruiser must be the boat Nate used for his island runs. She set her duffel and tote bag down and went back to the car for a plastic crate of cleaning supplies. The SUV was pulling out of the parking lot when she returned from moving the crate to the dock, and she entered the store more confidently this time.

"All set?" Nate asked, looking up from scanning her purchases.

"Uh . . . have you got any bacon? We always used to have bacon and eggs for breakfast at the cottage."

He laughed. "You'll be camping out, all right. How long since you've used a generator?"

"Not since the last time I was on Grand Cat," she admitted, "and Brian kept it going then. Should I take some candles?"

"Maybe a few, and I'll bring an extra tank of propane in case yours is low."

"Thanks. Is there anything else I'm not thinking of?"

"Bottled water?"

"Right, can't drink that lake water!" She hurried to get a twenty-four pack and set it on the counter.

As soon as he had rung up her purchases, Nate began loading the boat with boxes of supplies marked with the names of the customers. Emily recognized a few of them. "The Millers still have their cottage?"

He looked up in surprise. "Not the whole family. Just Raven."

"Oh?" Raven Miller was five years older than Emily and Nate, and had been known as the high school heartbreaker. Emily was surprised she hadn't ditched the small-town scene and never looked back.

"Yeah." Nate straightened and eyed her

with speculation. "I guess some things have changed since you left. Raven bought some more land from old Mr. Derbin a few years ago. She owns about six acres on the island now."

Emily stared at him. "I can't believe it. Mr. Derbin sold her six acres? I thought he wanted his solitude."

Nate shrugged. "So did everyone else. Maybe he needed the money, I don't know. But lots of people have been after him since to sell more property."

"What did Raven want with so much land? Did she subdivide?"

"No, she opened a retreat center."

"What?" Emily laughed, but Nate's face was sober.

"It's a women's camp of some sort. She calls it the Vital Women Wilderness Retreat. It's good for the town — brings in quite a bit of business in summer."

"What do they do?"

"I think Raven tries to give her clients the complete wilderness experience. They take kayaking trips up the lake and do a lot of snorkeling. Raven comes in to buy gear and organic food. And I think they do yoga and . . . I don't know . . . art, maybe?"

"Art?"

"She had me order a case of sketchbooks

and charcoal pencils this spring. I took a special speaker out to the island in my boat last weekend. She was . . . kind of strange. She talked all the way there about the empowerment of women."

Emily laughed at his discomfiture. "Well, I'll have to walk over and see Raven this week."

Nate swung her duffel bag into the boat. The door at the back of the store opened, and a pretty, dark-haired, middle-aged woman stepped out onto the dock.

"Emily! Nate told me you were here!"

Emily greeted Nate's mother with pleasure. "I'm so glad to see you, Mrs. Holman. And I'm sorry about your husband. I didn't know until today, but please accept my condolences."

"Thank you, dear." Connie Holman took Emily's hands in hers and looked her over from head to toe. "You've turned out very nicely."

Emily's cheeks warmed. "Thank you."

"How's your mother?"

"She's . . . well, my stepfather died recently, so she's having a bit of a rough time."

Mrs. Holman's features clouded. "Oh, I'm sorry. What happened to Brian?"

"It was his heart." Emily bit her lip. "They said he was under a lot of stress at work. I guess his heart just gave out. I . . . wasn't there when it happened. I live down in Connecticut, and . . . well, Mom's coping. She'll be all right, I think."

Mrs. Holman nodded. "I miss her. Maybe before you leave town you could give me her address? I'd like to send her a card."

"She'd like that," Emily said.

"I tend the store when Nate's out on the water. If you need anything, just let us know. Nate usually stops at Grand Cat at least once a day. Do you still have a boat out there?"

"Mom said there should be one in the boathouse at the cottage, with a ten-horse motor. She said the people who rented last summer used it, so it should be all right."

"I can check it for you," Nate said.

Emily nodded, glad for another reason to spend time near him.

His mother glanced up at the sky. "You'd better get going, Nathan. Those boys on Little Cat will want their care packages."

Nate loaded the two bins of mail and stood at the boat's rail. "Ready, Em?" He reached toward her, and she grasped his hand. His firm touch jolted her to her toes. She swung over the side, into the boat, and he grinned down at her.

"This is like old times."

She looked up at him. She didn't remember Nate being nearly this tall in high school. "Yeah, but I could look you in the eye then."

He laughed and cast off, waving at his mother.

Nate couldn't stop smiling as he guided the boat toward Grand Cat, the largest island in the lake. Emily was back! How many times had he wished for this moment? Seven years had passed, almost to the day, and she'd walked into the marina, just like that.

He looked over at her. Her blue eyes were wide and solemn, and her shoulder-length, honey blond hair flew about her face in the breeze. He eased off a bit on the outboard. No sense shortening the trip when the one person he'd longed to be with was in his boat.

"Do you mind if I stop at Derbin's first?" he called over the sound of the motor.

She shook her head. Old Mr. Derbin's cottage was isolated on the end of Grand Cat. He had owned the whole island at one time, but about thirty years ago had sold off a string of cottage lots on the end farthest from his own camp. The cottage owners were forbidden to trespass on his land, however, and his remaining property, about three-fourths of the island, was unoccupied. Raven Miller's retreat center was on the only parcel of land Henry Derbin had sold since.

Mr. Derbin lived on the island every summer. Even when Nate didn't have mail or groceries to deliver, he cruised by the dock on the end of the island, looking for the old man or at least for smoke from the chimney that served his fireplace. At seventy-nine, Henry Derbin was getting a little old to be living alone in such a remote spot.

Emily sat on the passenger seat, wearing a red life vest over her blue Windbreaker. She scanned the lake and its wooded shore with eager eyes.

"Glad to be back?" he asked.

She nodded.

He thought her cheeks were redder than normal, but maybe it was the sun. And her hair! Its golden luster was richer than he remembered. He couldn't resist catching a windblown lock and tugging it gently.

She smoothed it back, smiling at him.

"When did you cut it?" he asked.

"My freshman year of college."

He nodded. So . . . as soon as she left home, she'd cut off her long, golden braid. He wondered if she'd done it in a warped defiance of her parents . . . or rather, her stepfather. As far as he knew, Emily had never had trouble with her mother, aside from the fact that her mom had married the most pompous jerk in Maine.

He slowed the engine even more as they neared Derbin's dock.

"So, what are you doing in Connecticut?"

"Working for a newspaper."

He wasn't surprised, knowing her determination and persistence. She'd fulfilled her plan. Emily had always excelled at composition, and her parents had practically nursed her on printer's ink.

He looked toward Derbin's cottage. "The old man told me this will be his last summer on the island." Emily raised her eyebrows, and Nate added, "He says he's considering selling the rest of his property."

"To whom?"

He shrugged. "A lot of people are interested. All the cottage owners want more land, and some folks in town who didn't have the opportunity before would love to buy an island lot. Several groups would like to get hold of it, too."

"Oh?"

"Yeah." She was just so beautiful! At fifteen Emily had been more attractive than most girls her age, but she was quiet and kept away from the boys at the consolidated high school in Aswontee, the larger town they rode to on the bus. At eighteen she was distractingly pretty and still unattached. His best friend. But now . . . now her beauty almost took his breath away. *How did I let her leave? Was I really that stupid? She liked me. A lot.*

He swallowed and looked toward the wharf, judging the distance. "Then there's Raven."

"She wants more land?"

"Sure. I guess she wouldn't mind expanding. And there's A Greener Maine. Have you heard of them?"

Emily frowned. "No. Who are they?"

"It's an environmentalist group. And don't forget Camp Dirigo. The boys' camp is outgrowing its facility on Little Cat."

He cut the motor and eased the boat in next to the dock, stepping forward to tie up. "I'll run Mr. D's stuff up to the cottage."

Emily stood up, holding on to the back of her seat to steady herself. "Let me come with you. I'd like to say hello to Mr. Derbin."

"Sure."

She peeled off the life jacket and dropped it to the deck. Nate set the box of food and mail onto the dock and climbed up, then gave Emily a hand. He hefted the box, and they walked up the path together.

She looked around with shining eyes.

"I've only been on this end of the island a few times, back when I was a kid and one of my parents had a reason to go and see Mr. Derbin."

"It's a lot different from the other end of the island," Nate said. Mr. Derbin had a pebble beach, but most of his shoreline was rocky and untamed. His cottage was set back from the water on high ground that sprouted thick brush. Behind the little log house rose a craggy slope covered with evergreens. The old man had kept the buffer between his property and the other cottages. It was almost as though he still had the entire island to himself.

She turned and looked back down the path toward their boat and the rippling surface of Blue Heron. "What a view. I didn't realize how much I missed the lake."

"Doesn't your mother live near the ocean now?"

"Not really. I mean, you can't see the water from her house or anything." She wrinkled her nose. "You can smell the mud-flats at low tide. But here . . . well, at the house in Baxter we had a great view of the lake, and the cottage is right on the rocks, you know?"

Nate nodded, smiling at her childlike pleasure. "Did you go by your old house?"

She shook her head. "Not yet. The marina was my first stop in town."

They reached the doorstep, and he nodded for Emily to knock while he held the box.

"Your folks got one of the best lots," he said. "I always liked that cottage."

"Yeah, it's great. Just a little beach, but it's on the end of the row, so we never felt crowded." She looked anxiously toward the porch door. "Should I knock again?" Without waiting for his reply, she raised her fist and rapped again.

Nate frowned. "Usually he's on the dock when I come, or else he comes to the door right away. Oh, well. Maybe he went out for a walk." He shifted the box so that it rested against the doorjamb and tried the knob. "Nobody ever locks anything out here." He stepped inside and set the box down on the veranda. "I'll just leave it here for him."

"Maybe we should put his milk in the refrigerator." Emily stepped past him and peered inside the cottage.

"Mr. Derbin?" she called. "Hello! Mr. Derbin?" She gasped and stepped back, slamming into Nate. He caught her arms and pinned her against his chest for an instant while she regained her balance.

"What is it, Em?"

"Look!"

He stared past her into the next room. Henry Derbin lay on the floor, one hand stretched out toward them, a pool of blood spreading from his battered head across the linoleum.

2

Nate could feel Emily shaking.

"Easy." He pushed her gently aside and stepped into the kitchen, where Mr. Derbin lay. "He must have hit his head." Nate knelt on the floor beside the old man, fighting back the fear and nausea that gripped him.

"He's lost a lot of blood." Emily's voice held a tremor, and Nate glanced up at her.

"You okay?"

"Yeah. I'll call 911." She unzipped the pocket of her Windbreaker.

Nate felt for a pulse. When he looked up, she was fumbling with the buttons on her cell phone.

"Emily, he's gone."

Her face paled. "Are you sure?"

Nate winced and looked down at Mr. Derbin again. "Yeah, I'm sure."

She stared at the display on her phone. "What do we do? I'm not getting any reception."

Nate stood up slowly. "We're too far from any towers, and we're in a valley. About the only spot you might get reception out here is on that hill behind the cottage. But I've got the radio on my boat." He started toward the door.

"Wait," said Emily.

He turned, wondering if she was afraid to be left alone with the body. Her face was still sheet white, but she was frowning as she looked around the room.

"Nate, what did he hit his head on?"

He caught his breath, realizing she was right. There was no furniture near Mr. Derbin — nothing he could have fallen against except the floor. The blood pooled beside him, but there didn't seem to be any traces of it more than a couple of feet from the body.

"I don't see how he could have done it falling." Her voice shook, and he reached out to squeeze her arm.

"You're right." Leave it to practical Emily to think of that. He knelt on the floor again and forced himself to look at Mr. Derbin's wound. "It looks like something hit him really hard." He gazed up at her.

Emily stared back with those huge blue eyes. "Doesn't look like an accident," she whispered.

Nate stood and surveyed the room more carefully, looking for anything that might have been used as a weapon, but nothing seemed out of place.

"I'd better get out to the boat and make the call," he said. "No telling how long he's been lying here. Come on." He took her hand and drew her out through the veranda and down the path.

He helped her into the boat then used the radio to call the state police, giving the details of their discovery to the dispatcher.

"You're reporting an unattended death?" the voice asked.

"Yes, but . . ." Nate swallowed hard. "There seems to have been some violence."

Emily sat in the passenger seat watching him silently, biting her lip. As he waited for the dispatcher to contact an officer, he managed a reassuring smile.

"It'll take the unit thirty minutes to reach Baxter," the dispatcher said, "and they'll need transportation to the island."

"I can meet them at the marina with my boat," said Nate.

"No, the detective requests that you stay there to make sure no one enters the cottage until he arrives. Can you do that?"

"Yes. My mother is at the marina, and she can loan them another boat."

28

"All right, thanks. Someone will be there as soon as possible."

Nate put down the radio and grimaced at Emily. "Half an hour."

Emily leaned back and took a shaky breath. "Could be worse. At least they're not coming all the way from the state police barracks in Orono."

"I'm going to stay here," said Nate. "But you can take the boat over to your cottage if you want."

Emily winced. "I've never handled a boat this big before, and besides . . ." She gave him a sheepish smile. "I'd kind of like to know what happens."

He was glad she wanted to stay, even though he could tell she was shaken. For years he'd wished he could see her again and wondered if he ever would. It felt funny to be sitting so close to her after all this time. Finding Mr. Derbin's body gave the entire day a surreal cast.

"Do you have binoculars?"

"What?" He realized he'd been staring at her.

"Binoculars."

"Oh, yeah." He rummaged in a compartment beneath one of the seats and pulled out a black case.

"I thought maybe, if someone's still

around, I might see something." Her lower lip trembled as she took the case from his hand.

"Good idea."

She took the binoculars out and began to scan the shore, the tree line, and the lake. Gentle waves rocked the boat then slapped the dock pilings and the rocks on shore. Nate looked back toward the mainland. He knew Derbin's cottage wasn't visible from town. From the marina, he could see the peak of the roof with the aid of binoculars.

"Look for boats," said Nate. He gazed out over the water, squinting against the sunlight.

"I didn't notice many as we were coming out here. Just those two guys fishing off Moose Point."

Nate nodded. "I wish I'd paid more attention, but to tell you the truth, I was a little distracted."

Her lips twitched, but she kept the field glasses up and surveyed the expanse of the lake through them. "Do you think he lay there all night?"

"I don't know." Images of the dark blood on the linoleum came vividly to mind. They sat in silence for a moment, and Nate sighed. "Too bad this happened to him."

"Yeah." Emily lowered the binoculars and

looked at him. "I didn't really know him very well. He always seemed like a crotchety old man, telling us kids to keep off his land."

"He wasn't so bad once you got to know him," Nate said. "I've been sort of keeping an eye on him for the last couple of summers. He was all alone out here most of the time after his wife died, so I'd bring him his groceries and mail."

"Don't his grandchildren come visit?"

"Andrew usually comes for a week or two in July, but I haven't seen him yet this year. And Pauline never shows her face in Baxter anymore."

"Never?"

"Nope. I haven't seen her for three or four years." He eyed her with speculation. "Are you doing your reporter thing?"

She shrugged. "Can't help it, I guess. Don't you wonder what happened here?"

"Well, yeah." He glanced toward the cottage, unable to block out a mental picture of Mr. Derbin's corpse.

"Remember how Rocky Vigue used to follow Pauli Derbin around like a puppy dog?"

"Yeah." Nate chuckled. "Rocky's still in town, you know."

"I saw his father at the marina."

"That's right. Well, Rocky works at the paper mill. He's staying out here at the cot-

31

tage with his folks right now."

"Is his sister around? I wouldn't mind seeing Sarah again."

"She's married. Moved away."

Emily was silent for a moment, and the troubled look came back to her eyes. He knew she was still thinking about the body in the cottage above them. "Why would someone kill Mr. Derbin?"

"I don't know."

"Could it have been a robbery?" she asked.

"It wouldn't surprise me if he had a little cash, but I doubt he'd keep anything valuable lying around in the cottage." Nate scanned the bushes above the shoreline. Was a violent criminal here — on Blue Heron Lake? "There have been a few thefts in the area this spring, but it's mostly been at businesses, not houses."

Emily said, "People can be so wicked. Even here."

He sighed. "People are the same, no matter where they live. It's not the location that makes a difference in their hearts. It's knowing God."

"You're right." She sank back in her seat, the tension draining out of her shoulders. They talked quietly for the next few minutes, about the old days, the neighbors, and their families, but not about the old man lying dead in his kitchen a few yards away.

At last, a faint whir caught Nate's ear, and he reached for the binoculars.

"There's a boat leaving the marina now. The cops must be here."

A fifteen-foot boat carrying two men eased in next to the dock, on the far side of Nate's cabin cruiser.

A uniformed officer and a plainclothesman clambered out awkwardly. Nate jumped up onto the dock and helped lift their equipment onto the wharf.

"Are you Holman?" the man in jeans and a sweatshirt asked.

"Yes." Nate shook the man's hand. "This is Emily Gray. She owns a cottage on the other end of the island, and I was going to take her there after we left Mr. Derbin's things."

"I'm Detective Blakeney." He shook hands with Emily and turned toward the uniformed officer. "This is Trooper —"

"We've met." Nate grinned as he shook the other man's hand. "Emily, do you remember my cousin, Gary Taylor?"

Blakeney looked from Nate to Gary and back.

Gary smiled and nodded. "Hello, Nate."

He leaned forward to shake Emily's hand, favoring her with a crooked smile. "Good to see you again, Miss Gray. You've grown up."

Emily flushed but retorted, "So have you!"

"Where is the body?" Blakeney asked.

Nate pointed up the path. "In the cottage, sir. Would you like me to show you?"

"No, but if you and Miss Gray could wait here for a few minutes while Taylor and I take a look, I'd appreciate it. We'd like to get the full story after we examine the scene."

"Sure."

"We didn't touch anything in the cottage," Emily said.

Nate nodded. "Except that I did check for a pulse first thing. But he was . . . cold to my touch."

Gary pulled out a small notebook, consulted his wristwatch, and wrote something down.

Another boat approached from Baxter, and Nate squinted at it. "Here comes Felicia Chadwick, from the *Journal,*" he said to Blakeney. "Emily, do you remember Felicia?"

"Of course," said Emily. "When my mom owned the paper, she was the *Journal*'s ace reporter, and she bought it when Mom and Brian moved away. It's nice to know the

Journal is still going. And quick on the draw."

"You mean the press is here already?" Gary asked. "Man, they're fast."

"She must have heard the call on the scanner," said Nate.

"Well, she'll have to wait here," Blakeney said.

"I'll make sure she does." Nate returned Felicia's wave as she cut her engine and let her boat drift in to shore beyond the dock. "It's a weekly that comes out every Tuesday, so you can relax for a few days."

"Well, if the *Bangor Daily News* shows up, keep them away, too," Blakeney said, and Nate nodded.

The officers went up the path before Felicia could beach her boat and scramble out.

"It feels kind of strange to be so near a hot news story and not reporting on it," said Emily. "Normally I would be on the phone right now with my editor."

"This will boost sales for the *Journal*," Nate said.

Felicia approached from the shoreward end of the dock. Her camera was slung about her neck, bumping against her lightweight green fleece jacket. With her long limbs and white slacks, she reminded Nate of a birch tree coming into full foliage.

35

"Hey, Nathan!" She smiled brightly as she reached them. "I see there's a little excitement on Grand Cat today."

Nate smiled at her. "Is that so?"

"Come on, Nate. I distinctly heard a call for the medical examiner and the code for an unattended death on the scanner at the office."

"You don't miss much, Felicia."

She nodded. "That's my job." She glanced at Emily, then did a double take. "It can't be! Emily Gray, come home to Baxter?"

Emily stepped forward with a wan smile. "Felicia, I'm so glad to see you again."

The two women embraced, and Felicia fairly bubbled with excitement. "Are you here to stay?"

"Only for a week," Emily said.

"How is your mother?"

"She's all right. But my stepdad died. I don't know if you heard."

"No. Was it sudden?"

"Heart attack, last February. But Mom is coping. She'll be glad to learn you're doing such a great job here."

Felicia's face clouded, and she looked toward the Derbin cottage. "So just what happened here? The old man died?"

"You'll have to get that information from the officers," Nate said. "Sorry."

"Officers?" Felicia probed. "They sent more than one? What's going on here, Nathan?"

Nate shrugged. "It's just my cousin Gary and another guy. You know Gary?"

"Trooper Taylor? Sure."

Felicia had her notebook out and was scribbling. "Did you get the other guy's name?"

"Uh . . ." The name had slipped Nate's mind, and he wasn't sure they should give it out, anyway. He looked at Emily.

"She'll get it anyway, when they're done inside," Emily said. "Detective Blakeney."

Of course Emily had remembered. She'd always had a phenomenal memory. She'd put Nate to shame when it came to French vocabulary quizzes.

Felicia's pencil stopped moving. "Detective, eh?" Her eyes glowed. "I knew it! This is a front-page story. As soon as the *BDN* and the television stations hear about it, Baxter will be crawling with news crews. I don't suppose we can keep it quiet until I get this week's paper out." She pocketed her notebook and pencil and turned toward the shore. "I'm going up there."

"You can't," Nate said. "Blakeney specified that no one is to go up to the house."

"But —"

"They'll come down and brief you, I'm sure," Emily said.

Felicia nodded and focused her digital camera to get a shot of the cottage. "So . . . you two just happened along?" Nate and Emily said nothing, and the reporter looked around, her face pensive. "No, of course not. You found the deceased. I should have guessed it from the start. Tell me all about it."

"I . . . don't think the detective wants us to do that," Nate said.

"Oh, come on." Felicia turned to Emily and put on a wheedling tone. "Front-page interview in the paper your parents used to own."

Emily's lips curved and Nate's heart flipped. Amazing what one little smile from Emily could do to him. Was it because all these years he'd wondered if she was happy?

"Say, Felicia," he suggested, "why don't you interview Emily instead? Not about this. About her job in Connecticut."

"Oh, what are you doing in Connecticut?" Felicia turned to Emily, obviously suspicious that Nate was trying to divert her from the real story.

"I'm an investigative reporter."

"Really? You've got to tell me about it." Felicia cocked her head and looked at Nate.

"I know what you're doing, but it's okay. I'll get two great local stories today. The death of one of our oldest citizens, and the return of a beautiful young woman who went out into the world and clawed her way up the ladder of success."

Emily laughed. "That's a bit purple, don't you think?"

Felicia frowned. "Well, it's a feature, not a hard news story."

"Of course." Emily glanced at him, and Nate grimaced and shrugged. Emily seemed to understand. She took Felicia's arm. "Let's sit in the boat, where it's comfortable, for the interview. This will occupy us both until the officers come back."

Fifteen minutes later, Detective Blakeney came back down the path and took Nate, then Emily, aside to take their statements. He called by radio for more manpower and told Nate he and Emily could leave if they wished.

Felicia stayed in Nate's boat while Blakeney questioned them, but jumped forward when the detective's interviews were finished.

"I'm with the *Baxter Journal,* Detective. What can you give me?"

Blakeney sighed. "I don't have much for

you yet, but I can give you a few basics. You'll have to wait for the medical examiner's report to get a cause of death and so on."

"Come on," Nate whispered to Emily. He helped her into his boat and started the engine. She sat staring up at the cottage with a frown puckering her brow while he cast off.

"Think he's safe with Felicia?" he asked when they were a hundred yards out from the dock.

He was rewarded by Emily's chuckle, though the sound of it was drowned by the noise of the motor. "I think Blakeney can handle it. He looks as though he's dealt with eager reporters for the last thirty years."

Nate nodded. "I know Gary won't blab about anything confidential."

"They'll confirm that he's dead and not much more, probably," Emily said, pulling on the red life vest. "She knows we discovered the body, so she'll probably ask him to confirm that and fish for anything else she can get."

"Is that how you do it?"

She shrugged.

The run to the opposite end of Grand Cat took only a few minutes, and Nate tied up before the Gillespies' cottage.

"The dock looks a little worse for wear," Emily noted. "Is it safe?"

"Probably, but it wouldn't hurt to replace it with one of those new aluminum jobs before you get potential buyers out here to see it."

"I don't suppose the Baxter Marina sells them?"

"We do order them for special customers." Nate grinned as he swung her duffel bag onto the wooden dock and hefted the box of supplies.

"I'll mention it to Mom when I come in to the marina to call her." Emily placed her tote bag and sack of groceries on the boards then carefully climbed out, using the crude ladder at the deeper end of the dock. "You'd better get going. You're late with your mail run."

"I'll help you carry this stuff in. I wouldn't want to leave you and find out later you had no propane."

"Thanks." She picked up the tote and groceries. Nate got the other items and walked beside her up the gradual slope toward the cottage. Emily stared at the little house, and her eyes shimmered.

Halfway there, Nate stopped and looked around at the trees and boulders. Emily stopped, too, and turned toward him.

41

"What is it?" she asked.

"It was right about here, wasn't it?"

"What?"

"That I kissed you."

Emily's face went scarlet. She swallowed hard. "Yeah. It was exactly here."

He smiled, and she smiled back but couldn't hold his gaze.

"Come on." He walked ahead of her and set his burdens down on the steps. She held out a key, and he took it from her and opened the door.

He watched her face as she entered the cottage, stepping slowly onto the glassed-in porch, then into the kitchen, where she set her bags down on the old pine table. She walked to the door of the living room and surveyed the threadbare sofa, the fireplace of fieldstone, and the dusty shelves of books and games.

"Welcome back," he said.

She whirled toward him with an apologetic chuckle. "It's so small!"

"Yeah."

"And . . . rustic."

"Nothing's changed since your family used it summers."

She nodded. "I guess I've got my work cut out for me this week."

He followed her back into the kitchen.

While she unpacked her groceries, Nate checked the gas generator.

"You've got lights, and the stove and refrigerator are on now," he told her, "and I checked the plumbing. You should be okay for the week. Just remember, that hot water heater is small."

She grinned at him. "I remember. Quick showers. But not if you're planning to wash dishes soon."

"I'm so glad you're back, Em."

She looked down, still smiling. "Thanks. This day has been . . . not at all the way I imagined. But I'm glad you were here."

"Yeah. Too bad about Mr. Derbin. Emily, are you sure you're okay?"

"I'll be fine."

He hesitated. A murderer could be on the island. There must be something more he could do to make sure she was safe. He knew at that moment that he would be back before nightfall to check on her.

She stood on the dock waving as he headed out for the boys' camp on Little Cat, and Nate couldn't help thinking back to that night seven years ago. Their one kiss. He'd never forgotten it, and her flush when he mentioned it told him that she hadn't, either.

Her short-tempered stepfather had scared

him half to death that night. Nate had longed to see Emily again before she went off that summer. She'd gotten a job waitressing at some resort near the coast. It was supposed to pay well and make a good addition to her college tuition fund.

He remembered how he'd agonized those few days before she left, wanting to take the boat out to the island while her stepfather was off working at the paper mill. But he knew that if Brian found out he'd seen her again, he'd be angry. Nate decided that for his own good, and Emily's, he'd better abide by Mr. Gillespie's wishes. But he'd regretted that for seven years.

His heart raced, just thinking about her. Had she thought he was a coward when he backed down before her stepfather? Nate sighed as he pulled in at the dock on Little Cat. What did that kiss mean to Emily?

3

Emily made herself a sandwich for a late lunch. She spent the rest of the afternoon cleaning the bathroom and kitchen and wiping down the dusty lawn chairs. The grime was daunting, but vanquishing it gave her a deep satisfaction.

When she opened the kitchen cabinet nearest the sink, a wave of nostalgia struck her. Carefully she lifted down the loon-stenciled mug her father used to drink his coffee from.

Amazing this has survived, she thought. Her father had been dead fifteen years, yet the mug she gave him one Father's Day had come unscathed through his death, the stepfather era, and several years of renters at the cottage. She cradled it in her hands for a moment, then set it aside and reached into the cupboard, determined to sort through all of the dishes today to see if there were other items she or her mother would want to keep.

This has surely been a different sort of Saturday, she thought an hour later as she scrubbed away at the rust stain in the sink. The long drive from her mother's home in Brunswick, followed by her reunion with Nate and the discovery of the body, had sapped her energy.

The sound of an outboard approaching drew her to the porch just after four o'clock. Curiosity turned to anticipation as she recognized Nate's boat, and she ran down the slope to the rickety dock. He killed the engine and nosed the boat in, tossing her the painter, and she looped it over one of the posts at the end of the wharf.

"Thought you'd like an update," he said with a smile that would have melted a glacier.

"Great. Would you like to come in and have something to drink?"

He grinned. "Save your spring water. I made a pickup when I stopped back at the marina." He lifted a small cooler from the deck. "Still like root beer?"

"You remembered! Actually, I usually drink diet cola now."

"No problem." He opened the cooler so she could see the variety of soft drink cans inside. "I threw in some orange and ginger

46

ale, too, just in case."

"I scrubbed down a couple of lawn chairs that were on the porch," Emily said. "Want to sit out here?"

They settled in the shade of the big pines at the end of the dock, and Emily sighed with pleasure as she opened her can. "Ice cold. Thanks."

"You're welcome." He tipped back his soda and took a deep swallow.

"What's going on over at Derbin's?"

"Well, Blakeney called for a forensics team first thing. The medical examiner came about an hour ago, examined the body, and let them remove it."

"How did they get him to shore?"

"The game warden stationed in Millinocket brought a boat, and they're using that."

"So you didn't have to . . ."

"No. But I did shuttle the ME out when he arrived. He was sputtering about how he had to drive all the way up here from Bangor on a Saturday. I think they called him on the golf course. Oh, and Gary said they may want to interview us again. I told him we're not going anywhere. At least, I'm not, and you're staying awhile, right?"

"A week, anyway. It may take longer than I expected."

"There's a lot of traffic on the lake today."

"I'll say." Emily watched a boat zoom from the far end of Grand Cat toward shore. "I haven't seen so many cops on the water since Josh Slate drowned."

"Yeah, that was bad."

Nate sipped his root beer. "Have you thought about church, or would you rather just cocoon out here on the island tomorrow?"

"Do you still go to the community church?"

"Where else?"

She smiled. "Well, some folks do drive to other towns to go to church."

"We've got a great pastor."

"That's good."

"My mother thinks so, too." He winked at her.

"Am I missing something?" Emily asked.

"Yeah, maybe. Mom's been seeing Pastor Phillips socially for the last six months or so. I wouldn't be surprised to hear any day now that I'll be getting a stepfather."

Emily didn't know what to say. Her limited experience with stepfathers precluded her from congratulating him.

"He's a really good guy. And he likes fishing."

"That's . . . that's great."

Nate tilted his head to one side and studied her for a moment. "Did I tell you I'm really glad you came back?"

She chuckled. "You might have mentioned it. And yes, I'd like to go to church."

"Fantastic. I'll come out and get you around ten o'clock."

"Good, because I haven't been near the boathouse. For all I know, my outboard's a clunker."

"I forgot to check it over for you, didn't I? Maybe I can do that now — get your boat in the water for you and make sure that old Evinrude still runs."

Emily walked with him toward the little shingled building on the rocks. As they approached it, a huge bird rose from the reeds just beyond the boathouse. The noise of its wings flapping thrilled Emily. She and Nate stopped to watch as it soared high over the water with its long, sticklike legs thrust out behind it, and flew toward the wooded shore on the south end of the lake.

"Awesome," she breathed.

"I'll bet that heron is nesting in one of those old pine trees beyond that little marsh," Nate said.

She unlocked the door and peered inside. There was just room for the small aluminum boat. The two of them managed to lift it

49

down off the rack and lower it into the water. She watched Nate mount the motor and add fuel. It started on his first pull, and he gave her a thumbs-up then let it run for a minute or two.

"Want me to run it over to the dock?" he yelled.

She nodded, secured the door, then walked along the shore to meet him as he tied the small boat up beyond his cabin cruiser.

"You're all set." He climbed onto the dock. "You can putt around out here or zip over to Baxter anytime you want."

"Thanks! I guess I could take myself to shore in the morning."

"Don't even think of it. You already said I could come get you."

She nodded and smiled. If she kept looking into his eyes, her face would go all red again, she could tell. She sought a safe topic. "Well, you and your mom should have a lot of business for the next few days."

"Yeah. Blakeney said the state police will bring a boat of their own tomorrow, but they want to rent a couple from the marina, too, until the investigation is over."

"And there'll be reporters."

"Besides Felicia, you mean?"

"Well, yeah," she said. "This is the prob-

50

ably the biggest story north of Augusta all year."

He ran a hand through his windblown hair. "It's weird that Mr. Derbin's death is going to benefit the family business, you know?"

"Yes, but you shouldn't feel guilty. You'll help all the out-of-towners a lot by supplying transportation and groceries when they come to Baxter."

"I suppose. We can use the income, I know that."

"Maybe you should restock the soft drink cooler," she laughed.

"Was it hard going through your folks' old things and . . . remembering?" he asked.

She scuffed the toe of her sneaker against a crack between the boards of the decking. "Kind of. I found my old yellow plate. It's just a little plastic dish, but . . . well, Daddy used to make pancakes sometimes, and he'd pour the batter so it made an E in the pan, for Emily, then put the crusty, brown little E on my yellow plate for me. Those were the best times, Nate."

He nodded. "You miss him a lot."

"Hey, don't make me cry, all right? Even though I was ten when he died, I still get emotional. His death was tough, but Mom and I made it. We got through it together."

51

"Yeah. I always admired your mother. She's a strong lady."

She was grateful he didn't mention Brian, who had entered her life and her mother's three years after her father's death. She didn't want to think about the sad times. The cottage, for the most part, had been a happy place for her.

"It must have been hard when you lost your father, too," she whispered.

"Yeah, it was. We knew it was coming, but . . . You're never quite ready, you know?"

"I know."

He leaned toward her and hugged her swiftly, then released her. "Thanks, Em."

Her eyes tingled with a threat of the tears she'd tried to avoid. Finding Nate again had brought all her emotions to the surface along with layers of potent memories.

"I wish I'd known when it happened. Not that I could have done anything, but . . ."

"You were always a good person to have around when things were rough," he said.

Emily pulled in a deep breath, knowing she didn't want their time together to end. "Would you like to eat supper here? It won't be much, just —"

Nate grimaced. "Sorry. I'd really like to, but I promised Mom I'd be home. Pastor Phillips is eating dinner with us tonight."

He frowned. "I should have asked her if I could bring you."

"That's all right. I'm beat."

"She would have said yes."

Emily smiled at his plaintive observation. "She probably would have. But I'll see you in the morning."

A breeze came over the lake, rippling the water and ruffling their hair. Nate reached out and caught one of her locks, smoothing it back gently. "How about if I come over some evening and we have something to eat and play Monopoly?"

She grinned. In junior high their endless games of Monopoly had helped keep her mind off things at home. "You know I'd win."

"Oh, you talk big, don'tcha?" He ran his finger along her cheek and down to her chin. "I'll see you."

He hopped down into the boat. She stood on the dock and watched until he grew smaller against the far shore and the whine of the engine faded.

"Was that Nate Holman?"

Emily looked up to see one of her nearest neighbors, Truly Vigue, hopping over the rocks along the shore between their two cottages. Her classmate Sarah's mother was clad in brief aqua shorts and a cream-colored tank top. Although it was early June, she was already deeply tanned. *Florida vacation or tanning salon,* Emily thought. Truly's dark roots were showing, and she wore leather sandals, not a good choice for rock hopping.

"Yes, it was Nate."

"I should have come over quicker. I was hoping to send a letter to my daughter in to the post office with him. Oh, well. There's no mail tomorrow, anyway."

"I heard Sarah lives in Indiana," Emily said.

"That's right." Truly Vigue stared at her, then squeezed her eyes half shut, as though focusing on her more clearly. "Emily Gray."

"That's right. How are you?"

"Me? I'm fine. But what about you? Did you drop out of the sky?"

Emily laughed. "No, I arrived earlier today. Nate brought me out when he made his deliveries."

Truly shook her head. "Unbelievable. I never expected to see you again. You graduated high school, and *wham!* You were gone."

"Yes, you're right about that. This is my first trip back in seven years."

"Seven years. Imagine. Are you married?"

"No, but I understand Sarah is."

"Yes, and she's given me two gorgeous grandchildren." Truly looked at the letter in her hand. "I should have brought some pictures over."

"That's all right," Emily said quickly.

"I'll bring them tomorrow. You have to see them! Little Olivia looks just like Sarah did when she was two."

Emily nodded and wondered how she could gracefully get away.

"I was sending her news about the murder," Truly said, and Emily's attention snapped back to the conversation.

"Murder?"

"Did you hear about it? Old Henry Derbin was killed this morning. The police are over there now."

"Yes, I knew he was dead." Emily supposed it would have been unrealistic to think the other cottage owners wouldn't know. Her marathon cleaning that afternoon had kept her cloistered, but of course the others had noticed the unusual amount of boat traffic back and forth between Baxter and Grand Cat. Truly Vigue was known as a local gossip, even a decade ago. If anyone on the island had company, she knew about it. She was probably the first to welcome the renters at the Gillespie cottage each summer, and if a family invested in a new

55

boat, by sundown she and Marvin had the details, down to the manufacturer's suggested retail price and the discount given.

"Hey there, ladies!"

Emily looked over her shoulder and saw a white-haired man sauntering through the pines behind her.

"Are you the renter?" he called.

"No, Mr. Rowland, I'm Emily Gray. My mother owns this cottage. Remember me?"

"Emily — why, yes! Wiley Gray's daughter?"

"That's right." Emily smiled, pleased that he remembered her father's name.

Mr. Rowland joined them near the end of Emily's dock. "Your mother remarried, didn't she?"

"Yes."

Truly laid her tanned hand on his pale arm. "You remember — Brian Gillespie. The manager at the paper mill."

"Oh, oh, yes, that's right." Mr. Rowland nodded. "Never liked him. But I miss your father. Your real father, that is. He kept the property up nice." He glanced toward the cottage, and Emily tried not to cringe, as she could almost read his thoughts. It was true the place needed some repairs.

"What brings you here after all this time?" Truly asked, and Mr. Rowland waited for

Emily's response with the air of a spoiled house cat who's heard the electric can opener begin to whir.

"My mother's thinking of selling the cottage."

"Oh!" Truly grasped Emily's wrist. "How much is she asking? We're abutting owners, you know."

Mr. Rowland leaned in. "I don't suppose the Derbin family will sell some more land, now that the old man's dead."

"I . . . don't know," Emily said.

"I can hardly wait to see what his grandchildren do." Truly spoke with a tone of confidentiality, but Emily knew she would spread her views to anyone who would listen.

Mr. Rowland said, "I've been wanting to buy an acre or two behind my place for years, but Old Derbin wouldn't sell me any. Then he went and sold a piece to Raven Miller for that dingbat women's camp. Wouldn't you think he'd rather sell it to nice, quiet families?"

"Oh, the Vital Women aren't very noisy," Truly said. "They sit around on the rocks and meditate. But island property is hard to come by, and Marvin and I would love to add this lot to ours. The kids could use the cottage when they come to visit."

"Better sell it quick," Mr. Rowland said with a wink at Emily. "If the Greens get hold of it, it won't be worth a plugged nickel."

"The Greens?" Emily couldn't help asking.

"Those loonies from A Greener Maine," said Truly.

Something Nate had said jingled in the back of Emily's mind. "Do they want to build a park?"

"Worse," said Mr. Rowland. "Don't sell to them, whatever you do."

"That's right. They're buying land all over the state and turning it back to nature." Truly snorted in disgust.

"Back to nature?" Emily asked, a bit confused.

"That's right." Mr. Rowland pulled one of Emily's lawn chairs over and sat down. "They think people are evil."

"Not evil." Truly shook her head. "Just . . . intrusive. They think we should set aside land where people aren't allowed to go."

Mr. Rowland nodded. "They think people ruin a place just by going there. We don't want them to get a foothold here."

Emily probed her memory for what Nate had said. "Weren't they interested in Mr. Derbin's land before he died?"

"So they say." Mr. Rowland sighed. "If they buy up most of this island, we could all be forced to give up our property for a nature preserve."

"How could that happen?"

"Eminent domain." He nodded as if it were inevitable. "We landowners have been talking about it, and we're against it. We could lose our equity, not to mention our summer retreats. Don't sell them so much as one square inch, that's what I say."

Truly nodded. "We were trying to get all the island owners together to go and speak to Mr. Derbin about it and tell him we didn't want him to sell to A Greener Maine. If he wanted to sell the property, that was his prerogative, just not to them. It would hurt the rest of us."

"Was there any indication he was thinking of selling to them?" Emily asked.

"Well . . . a couple of bigwigs from that outfit came out in a boat a couple weeks ago."

"Did Mr. Derbin show them the land?"

"Hardly," Mr. Rowland said. "He yelled at them from the dock to go away. At least that's the way I heard it."

"Last Tuesday's *Journal* said the Greens were going to make Mr. Derbin an offer for his entire property on the island," Truly said. "But now that he's dead . . . well, maybe it will delay the process."

Mr. Rowland tapped his temple and winked at Emily. "Better sell your place quick."

4

That evening, Emily put away her cleaning supplies and headed out for a walk. Automatically she stared toward the north end of the island, where Mr. Derbin's cottage sat. She couldn't see far, as the shore bulged and curved between her family's property and his. Finding Mr. Derbin's body seemed almost like a dream now, but still vivid.

She shivered and turned in the opposite direction, on a path that ran behind the row of cottages. Through the trees, she glimpsed the water. The breeze ridged the surface with small waves. Farther down the shore, she heard yelling and splashing at one of the docks, and she ambled along in the shadow of the old pines.

The Vigues' cottage was the one next to hers. As always, Truly's domestic touches were evident, even from the back. Petunias bloomed in the planters on the back deck railing, and painted stones edged the path to their woodshed. The Rowlands' was next. Emily tried to remember the names of the owners of the other two cottages between theirs and the Millers', but drew a blank. She'd have to ask Nate.

After the last cottage, she rounded a bend and sighted a woman sitting on a large, flat rock near the water. She didn't move but stared out over the lake like the figurehead on the prow of an old sailing vessel.

Emily wasn't sure whether to go on or turn back. As if in answer to her concern, the woman slowly raised her head and looked at her.

"Hello. I didn't mean to bother you," Emily said.

"It's all right." The woman beckoned to her, and Emily stepped closer, off the path. "I'm Raven Miller."

When Emily was in junior high, Raven was one of the cool, older girls that the boys always chased. She pestered her parents for shopping trips to the Bangor mall, where she could find, if not the latest fashions, at least clothes more stylish than those available in Baxter or Aswontee. She'd kept her hair short and sassy, and creatively applied her eye makeup and nail polish with a free hand. Looking at her now, Emily hardly recognized her.

Raven sat cross-legged on the rock, wearing a pair of well-worn jeans and a T-shirt that faded through several shades of blue. Her long, dark brown hair was pulled back tightly. She wore no makeup, but a leather strand with polished beads circled her neck.

"I'm Emily Gray."

Raven nodded. "I thought you looked familiar. Your folks had the cottage on the far end. How long are you staying?"

"At least a week. I'm fixing up the place for my mother. She's decided to sell the cottage."

"I see. Well, you're welcome to visit Vital Women."

Raven nodded toward the woods beyond. "I live in my parents' old cottage, and I've built up quite a facility and enlarged the grounds. I have a staff of three. I'd be glad to show you around the camp sometime. I'm sure you'll find it fascinating."

Emily's curiosity overcame her wariness. "I'd like that. Maybe after the weekend."

"We offer wilderness outings and spiritual workshops." Raven leaned back, bracing her hands on the rock. "I find it very rewarding. We've been able to help a lot of women. We get them out here in the woods, away from civilization, and they realize there's a lot more to life than the rat race. I try to show

63

them that there's meaning and fulfillment within themselves and nature."

Emily wished she could express her own beliefs, knowing they ran counter to the ideas Raven put forth. Should she let Raven ramble on or tell her flat out that she didn't believe meaning came from within, but that true fulfillment could be found only in God?

Raven unfolded her legs and stood. "A woman's life should not be defined by her relationship to a man or her success in the corporate world. So many women can't get past that."

There's some truth to that, Emily thought. She wondered if God had any place in Raven's philosophy and decided to take Raven up on her offer of a tour during her stay on Grand Cat. Maybe then she could discover more about the young woman's beliefs and perhaps explain her own convictions.

"Did you hear about Henry Derbin?" Raven asked.

Emily gulped. "Yes."

"What do you know about it?"

"Not much."

Raven shrugged as if to dismiss the topic. "Well, it's good to see you again, Emily. Do stop by sometime when you're free. I've got some literature, too — a brochure on the

Vital Women Wilderness Retreat and some pamphlets on meditation and other disciplines."

"I'll do that."

Emily watched as Raven headed toward the trees. She couldn't help noticing how wiry and tough Raven had become — the same slender figure she'd always had, but now stronger and toned.

There was another way in which Raven hadn't changed. In high school, Raven had been "me" focused, demanding attention as her right. Although she purported to help others, she was still self-centered, talking about her own enterprise at length, but never inquiring about Emily's present life or the well-being of her family.

She smiled to herself. "Some things never change."

As she walked past the rock and down to the shore, she thought about Raven's camp and wondered what strange rituals were created there to build self-confidence and an unfounded sense of inner peace in the clients.

Inner peace. It was something everyone craved. With God's help, Emily had put to rest the bitterness she'd harbored toward her stepfather. Now other events troubled her. The memory of seeing Mr. Derbin's corpse, for instance. Would she ever be at peace with that image?

Dear God, she prayed, looking out over the water. *Please bring me peace, as only You can. And help me face all these people who want to know what's going on. I know You're in control. Help me to remember that You know what happened to Mr. Derbin, and what's going to happen in the future. And that You love me.*

The wind gusted, fanning her hair over her cheek. She brushed it aside and headed back to her cottage.

A half hour later, rolling back the quilt on her bed, she found she was more exhausted than she'd thought. She eased onto the lumpy old mattress, aware of the waves slapping the shore, and drifted off to sleep.

Nate woke early Sunday morning with a sense of anticipation. The marina was closed Sundays, and he usually slept in until it was time to get ready for church, but today was different. Today held Emily.

He grabbed a bite to eat and poked around the store, trying to think of a reason to head out to the island early.

His mother came over from their house next door in her bathrobe about nine o'clock and found him dismantling the fishing tackle display.

"What are you doing? I heard you go out an hour ago, and I thought you were just checking the boats."

He gave her a sheepish smile. "I did that, but I needed something else to do. I've been meaning to get those new lures out, and I have time now, so . . ."

Connie shook her head. "It's Emily, isn't it? She's got you all off kilter."

Nate was silent for a moment. "Maybe she has. Would that be so bad?"

"No. She's a wonderful girl."

"Woman."

"Yes, woman. I've always liked her, and I like what she's become."

He pressed his lips together. His feelings for Emily raged inside him, but he wasn't sure he was ready to talk about them yet.

"She's got quite a career going," his mother said.

"I know." Why did he think she would let him be part of her life again? Even though a current of long-suppressed attraction seemed to jump between them, she wouldn't stay here. He looked down at the box of swivels in his hand. "Mom, having her here . . . It changes everything."

His mother slouched against the door frame. "I knew you cared about her, but I didn't realize it went this deep."

He sighed, feeling empty and inadequate. "It's like . . . I don't know what it's like, but when I saw her again yesterday . . ." He shook his head, staring without focusing.

"You were both very young when she went away."

"I know. We were good friends all those years. But then, right at the end . . ." He gritted his teeth against the hurt of remembering. "You know what it's like? It's kind of like I rang the doorbell seven years ago, and I've been waiting for her to open the door ever since."

"Has she opened it now?"

"Maybe a crack."

She smiled. "Well, then, I'll be praying."

Nate fastened a red and white spinner to the display board. "Thanks, Mom."

The phone rang, and Connie stepped to the counter and picked up the receiver. "Baxter Marina. Oh, hello, Andrew. Sure, we'll have a boat ready for you tomorrow. Come in anytime. And I'm sorry about your grandfather."

When she hung up, Nate asked, "Andrew Derbin, by any chance?"

"You win the prize. He's driving up from Augusta tomorrow and wants you to take him out to the island." Connie ran a hand through her disheveled hair. "Well, I'm going to get dressed and put my makeup on, and then I'm going to fix breakfast. If you want to eat, come on over in twenty minutes."

"I had a leftover hot dog."

"That's not breakfast."

He finished mounting all the fishing tackle, put away the boxes, and marked the discontinued items for quick sale. When he went back to the house, his mother was dressed for church and heaping a plate with French toast.

He sat down and ate three pieces, but kept glancing at the clock on the wall over the stove.

"Relax," his mother said. "You have plenty of time."

Even so, he turned down coffee and went out to the dock, leaving for the island ten minutes before he had planned. The lake was a little choppy, but not bad. A ceiling of gray clouds hung low over Grand Cat. He pulled in before Emily's cottage and stood with one foot on the dock and the other precariously perched on the boat's gunwale while he tied up. The wind blew his hair askew, and his dangling necktie flipped over his shoulder.

"Hi!"

He glanced up and saw Emily coming down the path. Her blue sundress splashed a welcome bit of color on the dreary scene.

"Howdy." He climbed to secure footing on the dock and reached out to help her as she shifted her Bible and cardigan, preparing to descend into the boat.

"You look good."

"Thanks." The wind gusted, and she tried to hold her skirt down and not lose the items she was carrying.

"How are you doing?" Nate asked. "You got a pretty scary welcome yesterday. You okay?"

"I think so," she said.

"Good. On behalf of the town of Baxter, I apologize and promise you better things to come." He helped her into the boat. "Are sneakers the new thing?"

A blush stained her cheeks. "I didn't want to slip getting into the boat." She pulled a pair of leather sandals from beneath the cardigan.

"Ah. Smart thinking. One time I came out here on a Sunday to fetch a loose canoe that got caught up in some weeds. It was really windy, and I was afraid the canoe would blow off down the lake. I was at the far end of the island, and leaned over to grab hold of the canoe, and I fell in. In my Sunday suit."

Emily shook her head. "Not really?"

"Really. No one saw me except Mr. Derbin. He thought it was a riot."

She chuckled and took the seat beside Nate's.

"Better put that sweater on." He cast off and pushed away from the dock. "You sure you're okay?"

"Yeah, I'm fine. Oh, and I saw Raven Miller last night."

"What did you think of her?"

"She's changed in some ways. Not in others."

Nate started the motor. "Well, I have some news. Andrew Derbin called just before I left to come get you. He and his sister were notified of their grandfather's death, and Andrew plans to arrive in Baxter tomorrow."

"He and Pauline are the next of kin," Emily said. "That should keep Felicia busy."

"I expect so, if he'll grant her an interview."

Emily untied her sneakers and pulled them off, then put on her sandals. "What's going on with A Greener Maine?" Nate arched his eyebrows in question, and she explained, "Truly Vigue and Mr. Rowland

71

were talking about it yesterday. They said I should sell my piece of land as fast as I could so the Greens wouldn't try to take it."

"They're lobbying for legislation that will take land by eminent domain," said Nate. "They want to make a human-free preserve in northern Maine. I suppose all the islands, and even the shoreline, are vulnerable."

Emily's gaze traveled over the lakeshore. Outside the town limits, only a few buildings could be seen along the water. "Isn't most of the shoreline owned by paper companies right now?"

He nodded. "There are a few privately owned parcels, like the campground and Jeff Lewis's hunting lodge, but you're right. The paper companies hold title to most of it."

"So, if the Greens bought it up, they could force cottage owners out," she said. "And there wouldn't be any more vacationers in Baxter."

"Basically, it could wipe out the town."

Emily frowned. "Then my mother will definitely want to sell to an individual, not to A Greener Maine. She wouldn't want to help devalue other people's property."

"Seems like the best answer. We're all hoping the paper companies won't sell to them.

I'd hate to lose what we have here."

Nate knew a change like that would ruin the marina business. He and his mother would have to find other sources of income. "Right now, this is a tough place to make a living, but those of us who have been here a long time and understand the area can make a go of it."

"Yeah. But some things will change, anyway, after what happened yesterday. It's only a matter of time before the town is swarming with reporters." She sighed. "I wonder if this will make it harder to sell Mom's cottage."

"It's possible. On the other hand, I could see the news attracting enough attention for you to make a quick sale, if the Greens will stay out of it."

When they reached the marina, Nate's mother was waiting for them, and they drove to church in her minivan.

Nate watched Emily's face as they entered the small community church. She looked around, and a slow smile spread over her face.

"It's just like always."

Several people came to greet her, and she was soon immersed in small talk, catching the older residents up on her family's situation.

At the first lull, Nate guided her to a pew midway down the aisle, where his mother had settled.

"Feel like home?" he whispered.

"I'll say." Her blue eyes shimmered. "My church in Hartford is a lot bigger than this. I'd forgotten how nice it is to know everyone in the congregation."

Sitting beside her during the service put Nate in a pleasant turmoil. She seemed at peace, but he found himself on edge. He tried to make himself forget about her and concentrate on the sermon, but people kept looking over at them, and he felt his pride inching upward, just having her this close to him. A faint fragrance seemed to emanate from her hair, and he wanted to lean closer and smell it, but he couldn't do that. She and everyone behind them would think he was nuts.

After the service, the pastor insisted on treating them all to lunch at the Lumberjack, a restaurant just down the street from the marina. The pastor took Nate's mother in his car, and Nate drove with Emily in the minivan.

The Lumberjack's business boomed in summer, when boaters and campers thronged to the area, then provided a welcome rest stop for tourists the locals

74

liked to call "leaf peepers" during the fall foliage season. They were followed by hunters. In winter, snowmobilers kept the eatery busy.

"They still serve the best meatloaf on earth," Emily said with a sigh. Her plate held half the portion she'd been served.

The waitress offered dessert, but they all declined.

Nate looked out the window and said with regret, "I guess we'd better head out. The sky looks a little threatening."

"The weather report said thundershowers this evening," said his mother.

"You kids go ahead," Pastor Phillips said. "I'll see Connie home."

Nate and Emily went out to the parking lot. The wind was already starting to pick up, and Emily folded her arms in front of her, shivering as Nate unlocked the mini-van.

"It's gonna be a windy boat ride," he said.

By the time they reached the marina, the sky had darkened and thunder rumbled in the distance.

Nate took off his suit jacket and held it out to her. "Here, that'll help keep the wind off."

"Thanks, but you'll freeze now," Emily said. "I should have known enough to wear

75

a jacket."

"Yeah, you never can count on the weather on Blue Heron." He slipped it around her shoulders, over the thin white cardigan. The sweater was no match for the chilly wind that came off the water.

"You'll be cold," she said as Nate helped her into the boat. "Run inside and get another jacket."

He hesitated. "Maybe I'd better."

He ran across the dock to the back door of his mother's house and grabbed his Windbreaker. When he got back to the boat, Emily was sitting down and had removed her sandals, jamming her bare feet into her sneakers.

A fifteen-foot motorboat was chugging toward the dock, and Nate recognized Gary Taylor and another trooper in it. He walked out to the slip where Gary would tie up and waited for him.

"How's the water?" Nate asked, catching hold of the painter.

"Could be better." Gary reached out and pulled the boat against the side of the pier.

"I didn't think they'd have you working Sunday."

Gary shrugged. "The medical examiner says Henry Derbin died from blunt trauma. Blakeney sent Bob and me out to look for the weapon again."

"Did you find anything?" Nate asked, looking from Gary to the other man's face.

"No. We went over that cottage with a fine-tooth comb. We even beat the bushes outside, along the path. Nothing. Whatever the weapon was, the murderer took it with him."

They walked along the wharf as they talked, and Nate stopped beside the cabin cruiser. Gary eyed Emily with surprise. "Hello, Emily." She smiled up at them. "Are you two heading out? It's going to get rough."

"I'm just taking Emily out to Grand Cat," Nate said.

Gary nodded. "Well, we'll probably be back tomorrow morning. See ya."

Nate hopped down to the deck beside Emily and shoved off from the dock, heading for her end of Grand Cat. Emily wrapped his suit coat close around her, but her teeth chattered anyway.

"How'd you like the pastor?" he called over the engine noise.

"I like him. He and your mom make a good couple."

The hull pounded against each wave, and they gave up on conversation. When they reached the island, big drops of rain were beginning to splash into the lake.

"I'd better check your batteries and wood supply," he yelled over the wind as he boosted her out of the boat. "No telling how long this thing is gonna last."

Her eyes flickered. "I can do that."

Nate frowned. "Just trying to help."

"Thanks, but I'm not helpless."

"Humor me. I'm getting wet here."

They ran up the path and in through the porch. Emily took off his suit jacket and folded it over a chair in the kitchen. Nate headed for the woodshed attached to the back of the kitchen and made three trips to fill the wood box beside the fieldstone fireplace. On his last trip in, Emily was coming down the stairs wearing jeans and a sweatshirt.

"You didn't need to do that. But thanks. That'll keep me going for a couple of days."

"Let me start a fire for you," Nate said. "It's chilly in here."

"I can do it."

"I know you can, but I'd like to."

She scowled at him for a moment then shrugged. "All right."

He stooped to lay kindling and tinder in the fireplace. She was watching him, and he was suddenly nervous. What if he couldn't get it going right away?

Emily plucked the matchbook from the mantel and handed it to him. He struck a match and held it to the slivers of birch bark. The blaze took hold, and he breathed a sigh of relief.

"A one-match man." Her smile set his heart thumping.

"Haven't lost my touch."

He handed her the matchbook, laid a couple of larger sticks of firewood on the blaze, and stood up. Her smile had taken on a forlorn droop.

"You sure you're all right here alone, Em?"

He wished he could offer to stay awhile, but the lake would soon be so rough he wouldn't be able to get across to the mainland.

"I'll be fine," she said. "I'll lock the place up tight. You'd better go before the wind gets worse." The thought of the murderer still on the loose was never far from his mind. He considered offering to sleep on the couch, but he knew she would refuse.

"Okay, take care." He headed for the door, scooping up his suit coat on his way through the kitchen. She followed him onto the porch and stood watching while he sprinted to the boat through the downpour. He looked back before he ducked beneath the canopy. She was still standing in the porch doorway. He waved, then cast off and zoomed away through the whitecaps, straight toward the marina.

Emily was self-sufficient now, he knew. She'd been on her own for seven years, never returning home after high school for more than a short visit. Living alone and supporting herself, she had proven she didn't need anyone to take care of her.

But she was different from Raven and her friends. To hear them talk, you'd think men were unnecessary. To say a woman needed a man was slander in their hearing. But Nate couldn't help thinking that Emily needed someone. Yes, she could survive alone, but why should she, when sharing her life would bring out the tender, compassionate side he knew she possessed?

At least God was taking care of her, even if she wouldn't let anyone else.

5

Emily watched until the boat was tiny, then went into the kitchen and locked the door between it and the porch.

We never used to lock the door.

But with a murderer at large on Grand Cat Island, those days were over.

She fussed with the propane stove and put half a bottle of water in the teakettle to heat, trying not to think about the murder, but it kept intruding on her thoughts. She wanted to know what had happened, and why someone wanted Mr. Derbin dead. But that wasn't her job here in Baxter. Other people would dig around for the answers.

In the living room, she pulled a worn copy of *Jane Eyre* from the to-keep stack she'd set aside while cleaning. Perfect for a night like this.

The teakettle whistled, and she hurried to fix a cup of hot chocolate. Darkness came early, and the wind howled. Peals of thunder came closer as the heavy rain pelted the roof and sheeted down the windows.

Around six o'clock, she ate a quick supper by candlelight, then lingered with her book by the fireplace. After a while she found herself reading the same paragraph over and over, while her thoughts drifted back to Nate.

He was back in her life. For a few days, anyway. She didn't dare hope it would last. At the end of the week she would go back to Hartford. The cottage would sell, and she wouldn't have any excuses left to return to Baxter and see him again. Would he care?

At last she decided to go to bed, and she slept soundly for a couple of hours. Around eleven she was awakened by a boom of thunder. Rain beat down on the roof above her, and cold air seeped in.

She pulled her quilt off the bed and went down to the fireplace, carrying her flashlight. A bolt of lightning lit up the room, and a few seconds later thunder rattled the windows. She tossed some wood on the embers of the fire, sank into an armchair, and pulled her feet up beneath the quilt.

The image of Mr. Derbin's lifeless body and the eerie silence in his kitchen once again dominated her mind. It was no use trying to avoid those thoughts. She prayed silently.

What am I doing here, Lord? You've dropped me into the middle of something terrible, and I don't know why. I came here wanting to do a good thing for my mom and hoping for a few days of rest, and the first thing that happens is that Mr. Derbin gets killed. For some reason, You landed Nate and me in this. Why would You want that to happen to us?

She lay back and stared up at the rough board ceiling. She believed God had His hand in every phase of her life. He'd given her the desire to come back here. He'd placed Nate in her path. He'd allowed them to be the ones who discovered Mr. Derbin's body. Why?

She closed her eyes. Did it really matter why she was here? What mattered more was what she did, how she reacted. Amid all the turmoil in Baxter and on the island, could God use her for some special purpose?

And what about Mom's property, Lord? I thought it was simple. I'd come and clean it up, and that would be that. Now I find out it might be unmarketable if the legislature approves a nature preserve here. Mom might have to settle for whatever the state offers her.

She sat watching the flames for a long

time, cataloging the bad things that had happened in the last two days, from the murder on down to the strange reunion with Raven and the wobbly dock.

At last she felt the tension slip away. *I did believe You wanted me to come here, Father. I still believe it. Show me how You can use me here.*

And it wasn't all bad, she admitted. Good things had happened, too.

There's Nate. She couldn't help smiling as she remembered his bright eyes and wind-tossed hair. *Thank You for giving me that, Lord. I guess all the rest is worth it. I know You're engineering things, so I'll trust You to bring whatever is best into my life.*

The driving rain continued all the next morning. Emily set herself to one task after another until the kitchen, bathroom, and living room were spotless and she was weary of housework. In spite of the rain, boats ferried back and forth between Baxter and the far end of the island. She wished she knew what was going on. She was used to buttonholing police officers and asking for the latest news, but that wasn't her job here.

Just before noon, she upended a drawer from the desk in the living room, dumping the accumulated odds and ends out on the desktop. She tossed a couple of pencil stubs into the trash bag at her feet then stopped. A plastic identity badge lay among the jumble. Her stepfather's face stared up at her from his credential for the paper mill. Emily swallowed the hard lump that had popped up in her throat. Slowly, she reached for the plastic card that Brian had clipped to his pocket every day when he left for work. She turned his face away from her and held the badge over the trash bag, then released it with a shiver.

Time for a break, she decided. Definitely time for a break.

She made an egg salad sandwich and took it to the porch. The rain had slackened. She went outside and walked down to the dock. A light mist hung in the air, and a few big drops splashed down on her from the overhanging pines.

She strode to the far end of the swaying dock and turned to look toward the north end of the island. A boat was chugging toward Mr. Derbin's property.

"Hey, Emily! I heard you were here."

She turned toward shore and saw Rocky Vigue approaching. She recognized him immediately. Over the years he had grown from stocky to obese. The dock held as he stepped onto it, but she was suddenly afraid it would buckle under their combined weight.

"Hi, Rocky." She almost ran toward shore, but she couldn't pass him on the narrow platform. "Hey, let's get in under the trees. It's starting to rain again."

He stepped off the end of the dock to solid ground, and she hastened to lead him away from it.

"My mom said your folks are selling out." He puffed as he followed her up the path.

"Yeah, that's the plan."

"So, where do you live now?"

She stopped and faced him under the dripping trees. "Hartford." His blank stare led her to add, "Connecticut."

"Oh." He nodded. "You're not married, are you?"

She laughed. "Not even close. How about you?"

"Me? Oh, no." He looked down at the ground, shaking his head. His body shook with it. "Listen, we're going to barbecue later if it's not raining. Want to join us?"

Emily hesitated. "Who's *us?*"

"My folks and me."

"Well . . ." She glanced toward the next dock and saw that Marvin, Rocky's father, was out securing a tarp over his boat.

"Hello there, young Emily," he called,

waving at her.

"Hi, Mr. Vigue."

"Will you?" Rocky asked eagerly.

She gulped. "I sort of have a . . . a standing invitation in with Nate, if the lake's not too choppy."

"Oh." He frowned, and his whole big body sagged. "That's okay. Hey, do you know if they've arrested anyone for the murder yet?"

"Oh, I don't think so. It's early for that."

"I suppose. Man, I can't imagine why anyone would brain the old guy like that, you know?"

Emily winced.

Three women emerged from the trees behind her cottage and came toward them. Emily didn't think she'd ever seen any of them before. One was at least sixty, with loose, wrinkled skin and iron gray hair. The second was a decade or two younger, with hair bleached to an unnatural straw color. The third was no older than Emily, with lithe, tanned limbs and a smile that reminded her of their top advertising saleswoman at the newspaper. She could sell anything. All wore white T-shirts emblazoned with green lettering spelling out "Vital Women Wilderness Retreat."

"Hello," called the youngest woman as they all came closer.

"Hello," Emily replied in dubious greeting.

"I'm Jenna, and I'm from the retreat center. These are Lillian and Shelly, two of our guests this week."

Emily introduced herself, and the women seemed already acquainted with Rocky.

"Isn't it awful about this murder happening here on the island?" Lillian, the gray-haired woman asked.

Emily murmured, "Yes."

"It's got everyone at Vital Women on edge," Shelly said. Emily immediately pegged her distinct accent as Upper West Side. "We all wonder if the killer will strike again."

Jenna's white teeth gleamed as she smiled reassuringly at the two older women. "We've advised our guests to stay in groups if they leave the lodge."

Lillian grinned. "Here's our group. One, two, three. Three's a group."

Shelly and Jenna laughed.

Emily smiled, trying not to grit her teeth, certain that if Nate couldn't get across the water tonight, she'd go crazy.

"I wonder if it had anything to do with him saying he'd sell his land," Jenna said.

"That was just a rumor," Rocky told her.

"I don't think Mr. Derbin would really sell it all."

"Well, he was getting old," Jenna countered.

"Emily!"

She turned and saw Truly and Marvin coming along the shore from their dock.

"Emily, have you heard anything more about the murder today?" Truly called.

"No."

"Too bad," Truly said. "I thought you might, since you're a reporter, and you went off with Nate Holman yesterday."

"We went to church," Emily explained.

"Church?" Shelly, the New Yorker, said. "Where? On shore?"

"Yes. There's a —"

"We don't need church," Lillian put in. "We spent hours chanting yesterday. The lake was too rough for snorkeling, so we had an art class in the afternoon."

"That must have been . . . interesting," said Emily.

"Oh, it was. I designed an icon depicting my soul at rest."

Emily tried to picture that graphic, but gave up.

"Do you think Old Man Derbin's family will sell his land now?" Jenna asked.

Emily frowned at her callousness, but no

one else seemed to mind.

"Wouldn't that be something, if the kids decided to subdivide," Marvin said.

Shelly looked along the line of cottages. "Prices would be high."

"Probably," Truly agreed, tugging at the hem of her damp shorts. "But if it's not too high, we'd love to have a little more land. In fact, Emily, on the next good day, Marvin and I plan to go over to Blue Heron Realty and speak to Bridget about your property. This would really be the ideal addition for us."

Jenna nodded, scrutinizing Emily's temporary abode. "Raven mentioned that this end cottage was for sale."

Marvin said, "Well, if Mr. Derbin had lived, he probably would have sold his land all in one piece."

"Oh, I don't know," Truly countered. "He's sold small parcels before. He could have sold several more lots and still kept his own cottage if he wanted to."

"I wonder if the boys' camp will try to buy it from the grandchildren now," Marvin said. "You know Rand Pooler, Emily?"

"I . . . vaguely remember him. He was ahead of me in school."

"He was in my class," Rocky said. "He runs the boys' camp now."

"Yes, and he told me they really need more space," Marvin said. "The state requires them to have a certain amount of square footage per camper in their cabins, and they want to add some new facilities, but of course their plumbing is primitive. They'd really like to move to a bigger piece of property."

"You can't put dozens of screaming little boys on this island." Jenna's lip curled in distaste. "We'd lose our ambiance of serenity."

"Yes," Lillian said with a frown. "Vital Women couldn't coexist with boys."

"Those Greens are trying to raise money from the big environmentalist outfits," Rocky put in. "If they get hold of Grand Cat, none of us will exist here anymore."

Truly nodded. "They're trying to raise money privately to buy land, in case they can't convince the legislature to approve their proposal for a wilderness preserve backed by tax dollars."

"Barton Waverly was out here last month," said Marvin.

"Who is that?" Lillian asked, brushing at her gray hair to drive away a mosquito.

Jenna said, "He's the president of A Greener Maine."

"He lives over in Aswontee," said Truly.

"They say he came out here in a boat with a reporter from the *Bangor Daily News,* looking over the island and talking about the Greens' plans."

"I hope they won't buy this whole island." Lillian's voice quavered as she stared at Jenna. "We could lose our lovely camp."

"That's even worse than being overrun by little boys," Shelly agreed.

"Well, we're going to do everything we can to prevent anything like that happening." Jenna, the young Vital Women staffer, put on a cheery smile. "You've been coming here for three years now, Lillian, and we're all going to be here for a lot more years."

Shelly nodded. "Raven will see to that."

"Well, I'm not sure I would have come this week, if I'd known there was a murderer lurking about." Lillian's voice quavered, and she looked over her shoulder up the path.

"Who's that?" Jenna asked suddenly, and they all followed her gaze out over the water.

Emily saw a boat puttering toward them from the mainland. She hoped desperately that it was Nate, coming earlier than she'd expected, and that he would rescue her from the impromptu gathering. But her anticipation took a nosedive when Truly said, "It's the Kimmels."

"You know them, don't you, Emily?" Marvin asked.

"I don't think so."

"No, they came after she left," Truly told him. She turned to Emily. "They bought the Jacksons' cottage a few years ago. They have three sons, and they'll stay all summer, until Labor Day weekend. Their boys aren't so bad. Once in a while they get noisy, but for the most part they're all right."

"Well, I let their father know the first year they were here that those kids needed to be quiet from nine p.m. to nine a.m." Marvin gave an emphatic nod.

The Kimmels' boat made straight for their private dock, and it was soon hidden by the irregular shoreline.

"Goodness, this pier needs some attention, Emily!"

She looked toward Marvin and saw that he was gingerly poking the end of her dock with his foot.

"I'm thinking of replacing it," she said. *Lord, give me patience.*

Truly nodded. "You probably should."

"I suppose we should go back," Lillian said, eyeing Jenna. "I hope those policemen find out where the murderer is soon."

"Not on this island, I hope." Shelly shivered.

"Well, I don't know about that." Marvin

pursed his lips for a moment. "There wasn't much boat traffic Saturday. Seems to me it's likely it was someone out here on the island that killed the old man."

"What a horrible suggestion," Lillian murmured.

"Well, if a stranger came out here in a boat, someone would have seen him," said Truly.

"Not necessarily." Marvin turned on her, ready to argue. "If someone came from the state forest land on the west side of the lake, we wouldn't be able to see them from this side. They could go right around to Derbin's cove and anchor without being seen."

"We'd have known," Truly insisted. "It was calm Saturday. We'd have heard a motor."

"They got a new crop of boys on Little Cat Saturday afternoon," Rocky said. "Who would notice one more boat?"

"That was after the murder." Truly glared at her son. "The police said it happened early in the day, didn't they?"

Marvin said, "You came Saturday, Emily. It happened before you came, didn't it?"

"I . . . well, yes."

"I certainly hope there's not a murderer loose on this island among us." Lillian's voice was hushed in fear.

"Excuse me," Emily gasped as the rain

began once more to pound down on them. "I think it's time to take cover."

She ran up the path to her cottage and dove through the porch door. Turning to look back, she saw the Vital Women flitting into the trees and the Vigue family rushing toward their cottage. Rocky lagged behind and looked up toward Emily and waved. He seemed to be waiting for a response, so she waved back. He turned and waddled after his parents.

She stood behind the glass-paned door and watched the rain streak down, forming rivulets on the sloped path and carrying pine needles and earth toward the lake.

On the next good day, I'll go ashore, she decided. At the Baxter town office, she could look up the names of all the people who owned property on Grand Cat. Nate would take her. But no. Why bother to ask him when she could take herself? In Hartford, she wouldn't consider asking for help. She'd just go do the legwork on her own. But she knew she wanted to spend time with Nate while she had the chance.

He'd probably like to help me with the research. We could look into it together. She felt the excitement that always came to her when she started a big new investigative story. *I'll find out who all the landowners are and how many of them were here on Saturday.*

Nate had wanted to be a policeman, and it must frustrate him to see Gary in the thick of it while he was still a bystander, running the marina. Of course he'd enjoy digging into the islanders' backgrounds with her. But if she and Nate worked together, they might find some connection between one of the landowners and Henry Derbin, other than the simple sale of cottage lots a generation ago. A reason for someone to be angry with him. Angry enough to kill.

6

There were few customers at the marina that afternoon. Every now and then someone from the mainland came in for a newspaper or a jug of milk, but there wasn't enough business to keep Nate occupied for long.

He kept thinking about Emily and the murder, and hoping she was safe. There was no guarantee the murderer wasn't still on the island, maybe one of the summer residents. This worried Nate more than he wanted to admit, but he didn't want to say so to Emily. He didn't want to frighten her.

By three o'clock, he was fishing for something to do. On any other day he would have closed up early, but Andrew Derbin was still due to arrive and would need a ride out to the island. To kill time he counted down the cash drawer, swept the floor, and washed the front windows. He'd just started wiping down the refrigerated case when the front door creaked open.

"Howdy."

Nate turned as Andrew entered, looking around the store. He hadn't changed much; tall and lanky, with short, blond hair. Nate remembered longer, disheveled curls when Andrew was in high school, except in basketball season. The coach made the boys keep a clean-cut image back then. Andrew had kept his trim athletic figure, though he now held a desk job in Augusta.

"Hey." Nate stuffed his rag in the pocket of his jeans. He stepped over to Andrew and extended his hand.

"Hi, Nate, good to see you again."

"You, too. I'm sorry about your grandfather. We sure will miss him around here." Nate stooped to pick up the bottle of window cleaner and took it behind the counter.

Andrew followed him. "It still hasn't sunk in, you know? My sister and I spent a lot of summers on the island with him and my grandmother over the years. Lot of memories tied to this place. Hard to believe he's gone."

"Yeah. It's rough when it's unexpected." Nate turned to take the key to the boat from a pegboard behind the cash register.

"You're never really ready for someone to

go. Makes me wish I'd spent more time with him."

"That's how I felt when my dad died," said Nate. "But I think feeling that way just means you really loved him."

Andrew frowned. "That's what I don't understand: Who could possibly hate my grandfather enough to kill him? Unless it was a robbery. But if it was, they sure didn't take much."

"I didn't realize anything was taken." Nate's thoughts began to rush. Maybe Mr. Derbin had kept valuables or antiques in his cottage, and someone had found out. Or maybe he had a secret stash of money, Silas Marner–style.

"Nothing much." Andrew leaned against the counter. "The police mentioned he didn't have a wallet on him when they asked if I thought anything was missing."

"That is odd," said Nate. "Did your grandfather tend to carry a lot of money?"

"Not that I know of." Andrew picked a cheap compass out of the bucketful beside the register, looked at it, then put it back. "But there's no telling. I mean, I never really thought about what he kept in that cottage until now. Things could be gone, and I wouldn't have a clue."

"True," said Nate. "And I don't suppose

most people would bother to carry their wallets unless they were leaving the island that day. Well, you got more gear in the car? I'm ready to head out whenever you are."

Andrew nodded. "Yeah, just a few things. I can handle it."

"Let me get my junk." Nate grabbed an insulated lunch box from under the counter, went to the refrigerator case, and slid the steak he'd been saving for supper with Emily into the lunch box. Then he took his jacket from the peg by the door and grinned at Andrew. "Okay, let's go."

Nate locked up the store and followed Andrew to his pickup truck across the parking lot. The sky was still gray, and it was sprinkling.

"It's just a suitcase and sleeping bag." Andrew reached into the bed of the truck for his luggage.

They'd started down to the dock when a car pulled into the lot and Felicia Chadwick jumped out.

"Hello, Nate!" She was wearing her camera around her neck and carrying a notepad and pencil, never without the tools of her trade.

"Hi, Felicia," Nate called back. He waited for her to catch up. "This is Andrew Derbin. Andrew, you remember Felicia Chadwick.

She runs the *Baxter Journal* now."

Andrew nodded. "How you doing, Felicia?"

"Great. Let's see, Andrew, you live in Augusta now, right?"

"That's right. I work in the secretary of state's office."

"Impressive. Hang on a second." Felicia backed up a few steps, lifting her camera. "Hope you don't mind." She snapped the picture before Andrew could say whether he minded or not. "Thanks!"

Nate stifled a laugh. "No one could accuse you of slacking on the job, Felicia. But it beats me how you always know when to show up for a news story."

"I called your mom." She gave him a sly wink. "So, Nate, anything new? I've got to have something to put in the next edition."

"Don't you have tomorrow's *Journal* written yet?"

"Of course. It's already at the printer's. Now I'm looking for my lead story for next week. Don't hold out on me."

"I don't really have anything new."

Felicia shook her head. "I'm not sure I believe that. How about you, Andrew? Do you have anything to say about your grandfather's death?"

Nate started to protest, but Andrew gave

her a weary smile. "My grandfather was a good man."

Felicia began writing on her notepad.

"I was really angry when I heard he'd been killed. It seems utterly pointless to kill a nice old guy like Grandpa. All I have to say is, the murderer won't get away with this."

"Won't get away with this," Felicia repeated as she wrote. She looked up. "Have the police interviewed you?"

"Yeah, sure. They talked to me and my sister, Pauli, on Saturday. They asked me to take a careful look around when I go out there today."

"Why is that?" Felicia's eyes glittered.

"They want to know if I think anything is missing."

"So, they think it was a robbery?"

"Maybe. They didn't find his wallet — no driver's license or anything lying around. Seems like that should have been in the cottage, but they didn't find it."

Felicia continued to take notes. "So was anything else stolen?"

Andrew shrugged. "Well, I haven't been out to the island yet. And we don't know that his wallet was stolen. Maybe he left it at home when he came up here last week to stay at the cottage."

102

She scribbled frantically and flipped a page in her notebook. "This is great. It will really help my story along."

A black Toyota Prius pulled into the parking lot. The driver parked askew across two of the places closest to the marina door.

"Who is that?" said Felicia, scowling.

"I don't know," said Nate. "Guess I'd better stick around and find out."

A tanned middle-aged man with graying blond hair emerged from the vehicle and strode toward them.

"Andrew Derbin," the man said, extending his hand as he reached them. "I'm Barton Waverly, president of A Greener Maine."

Nate wrinkled his forehead. Should have guessed it from the classy hybrid car. Alternative fuels . . . wilderness refuge . . . He was probably a vegetarian, too.

Felicia's eyes got wide, and she flipped her notepad open again.

"Hello." Andrew eyed Waverly coldly and made no move to shake his hand.

Waverly pulled his hand back. "Mr. Derbin, I heard you were arriving in town today, and I wanted to speak to you. Are you planning to sell the land your grandfather owned?"

"No, I'm not," said Andrew. "My sister and I have absolutely no intention of selling to you."

Waverly frowned. "Is that definite?"

"Yes, it is."

Felicia scribbled furiously.

"That piece of land's worth a lot to A Greener Maine," Waverly persisted. "I'd be willing to give you twice what it's assessed for. You can't refuse that kind of an offer."

"I already have. Excuse me." Andrew turned and walked on toward the dock.

"Now just a minute." Waverly hurried after him.

"I'm not interested!" Andrew did not look back.

Nate stepped between Waverly and Andrew's retreating figure. "You'd better take off. I'm taking Mr. Derbin out to his grandfather's property, and he'd like some time alone."

Waverly's face was beet red. His forehead glinted with sweat just below his hairline as he shoved Nate aside. "Keep out of this. I'm not talking to you."

Nate teetered and regained his balance. "Hey, watch it, buddy! You leave right now or I'm calling the cops, and they're not far away."

Felicia held out her cell phone to him. "Be my guest, Nate. It will make a great photo for the front page when they arrest Mr. Waverly."

Waverly glared at them then shot a regretful glance toward Andrew, who was climbing into the boat. "He'll change his mind," he muttered, and pivoted toward his car.

"And next time, would you park straight?" Nate called. "We need to keep those spaces open!"

Felicia laughed. "Now that's what I call a juicy tidbit."

Thunder rumbled in the distance.

"I'd better move. Take care." Nate sprinted for the dock.

They reached the island just before a new downpour broke. Andrew hoisted his luggage and ran toward Mr. Derbin's cottage. Nate motored the length of the island and secured the boat at Emily's dock, grabbed the lunch box, and hurried up the path.

Emily opened the porch door wide for him. Her cheeks were flushed, and in her cream pullover sweater and faded blue jeans, she looked warm and welcoming.

"Hey there." Nate shook the drops off his Windbreaker. "I dropped Andrew Derbin off at his grandfather's, and thought I'd stop by."

"Come on in," said Emily. "It's freezing out there. What's in the cooler?"

"Well, since it's dinnertime, and the last time I was here I personally took inventory of your food supply, I kinda thought you might like a steak. If you don't mind me inviting myself to dinner, of course?"

She smiled as she shut the door between them and the storm. "Not at all. And I was getting a little tired of sandwiches. Why don't you make yourself at home while I cook?"

"You sure you don't want any help?"

"Nate, I don't remember your knowing how to cook. Of course, it's been a long time."

"A long time since I burned the macaroni and cheese and ruined my mom's best saucepan?"

She grinned. "Well, that wasn't exactly what I meant."

"You're right, though. I still can't cook." He handed her the cooler and peeled off his jacket.

"I'm surprised they're letting Andrew stay at Mr. Derbin's cottage," she said.

"He says they're done collecting evidence out there."

Emily's eyebrows drew together. "I suppose they're waiting on the autopsy and the reports from the crime lab, but still . . . Did Gary say anything to you? Have they got anything solid in this case?"

"Not that I know of."

By the time dinner was ready, it was dark outside. The thunder stopped, but the rain still beat heavily on the cottage roof. They ate at the pine kitchen table, and afterward Nate offered to help her with the dishes.

"It will only take me a minute." She ran hot water into her dishpan.

"Well, then, how about I bring in some more firewood?"

She frowned. "I'm not a delicate piece of china, Nate. I can carry my own wood in."

Nate winced and wondered if he was stepping on her independent toes again.

"I'm just trying to help, Emily. It wouldn't kill you to let a friend do something for you and just say thanks. It makes the other person feel useful, you know?"

She shrugged. "Well, the wood box is getting low."

He brought an armful of wood in and stoked the fireplace, then pulled two armchairs closer to the heat. A few minutes later, Emily came from the kitchen to join him.

She curled up in one of the sagging, overstuffed chairs, and Nate sprawled in the other. For a moment there was no sound except the rain on the roof.

"I used to love that sound," she said, "but I'm getting kind of tired of it now." Her face glowed in the warm firelight.

Nate nodded. "I keep hoping it will blow out to sea."

They sat in pleasant silence for a moment. Just being with her satisfied a craving he didn't know he had. Did she feel that, too, or was she happy with her self-sufficient lifestyle?

"Hey, did I tell you there's a television news crew from Bangor staying at the Heron's Nest?" he asked at last.

"The bed-and-breakfast?"

"Yeah. The cameraman came in the store this morning for a case of soda."

"I hope they don't want to interview us. I mean, since we found Mr. Derbin."

"I thought of that," said Nate. "They came around and talked to me for a while at the store, and I thought they'd rent a boat to come out here and take pictures of Mr. Derbin's cottage, but I guess the rain discouraged them. And I didn't mention you."

"I appreciate that. The whole island is talking now," said Emily. "I can hardly get away from it. Oh, and I saw Rocky Vigue today."

"What did he have to say for himself?"

"He asked me if the police had made any arrests. And then three of the women from Raven's camp were out walking and joined in with questions about the land, all full of drama about the danger to the island people. And Truly and Marvin had to put their two cents in. Marvin thinks it was someone on the island. At least he does until Truly agrees. Then he changes his mind."

Nate laughed. "Well, it seems likely to me."

"Really?"

"It makes sense. Someone who knew the old man was there alone. This wasn't random, Em."

"But . . . someone could have come out from the shore without being noticed."

"Yes, there are ways of getting to the island without being seen."

"Marvin mentioned that, too. He said someone could easily have come from the west side without being seen. But then Truly said they would have heard a motor."

"If there was a motor," said Nate. "You'd be hard pressed to row against the wind now, but on a calm day . . ."

"Just a minute." Emily got up from her chair and disappeared into the shadows beyond the range of the flickering firelight.

"Let me get a notepad."

When she returned, Nate saw the enthusiasm on her face.

"Let's make a list of all the people who might benefit from Mr. Derbin's death," she said. "Suspects, motives."

"Shouldn't we leave that to the police?"

She wrinkled her nose. "Oh, come on, Nate! You wanted to be a cop. But the police won't tell us anything. Aren't you dying to be in on this investigation?"

"Like you are?"

She frowned. "Okay, so I'm curious."

"It's your job."

"Well, yeah. I'm trained to dig into things like this. It *is* my job to uncover the truth and tell people about it. Does that bother you?"

"Well . . . I'm not sure."

They glowered at each other. It stung a little that she'd brought up his career failure, while she'd succeeded at hers. *I'm not jealous of her,* he thought. *Or am I?*

He laughed. "Maybe it bothers me more than I've admitted. Let's make that list."

Emily smiled and settled back with the notepad on her knee.

"First there's the obvious," she said.

"His grandchildren?"

"Andrew and Pauline will probably both

inherit the land, don't you think?"

"It sounded that way when I talked to Andrew earlier," Nate said. "Their father died several years ago."

"Where's their mother now?"

"She remarried. Moved out west, I think. I doubt she'd be an heir."

Emily wrote down the names. "Okay. Who else?"

"Barton Waverly."

"Someone mentioned him today, too." Emily kicked her sneakers off and tucked her feet under her in the chair. "They said he came out to the island recently with a reporter to talk about the land."

"Yeah, and he was nosing around today."

Emily looked up. "You don't seem to like him much."

Nate shrugged. "He seems a little slick. Dresses like an outdoorsman, but . . ."

"But not a real outdoorsman?"

"I don't know. I think I've seen his clothes in the L.L.Bean catalog. You know, like he's ready to go trek the Appalachian Trail, but you know he's never walked farther than the coffee machine in his life. And he drives one of those hybrid cars, too."

Emily smiled. "Politically correct and ready for photo ops."

"He caught Andrew and me just as we

were ready to launch."

Emily began writing on the notepad.

"He wanted to know if Andrew was interested in selling." Nate shook his head at the memory. "Andrew said there was no way he and Pauli would sell to him, and Waverly got angry. I had to chase him off. Felicia was there, too, so that'll be in the paper. I'm afraid I didn't handle it very well, Em."

"We'll see how Felicia portrays you next week." She was still smiling, and her face had softened and lost the skepticism. "So, Mr. Derbin's death seems to have delayed the sale of the land."

"Yeah."

"You know, people out here are saying Mr. Derbin was considering selling the land, or parts of it, and it seems everybody wants a piece. Which reminds me, Vital Women and Camp Dirigo were mentioned as potential buyers." She wrote on the notepad again.

"Makes sense. They need more space."

"But how does that relate to the murder?"

Nate tried to piece that together without success. "Maybe someone made him an offer, and he turned it down."

"But would they be mad enough to beat his skull in?" Emily winced.

"The Vital Women might be that passionate."

112

"I don't know. Raven seemed emotionally flat when I talked to her. But the Greens . . ." She arched her eyebrows. "They can be fervent about their cause."

"It wouldn't surprise me if they sank to violence on occasion," said Nate. "Maybe they'd commit murder to stop the land from being developed, if they thought Mr. Derbin was going to divide it up into more cottage lots."

"I still don't see how killing him would help." Emily chewed the end of her pen.

Nate stretched his legs toward the fire. "I have to agree with you there. If he was thinking of selling his property, but his heirs aren't, then whoever killed him worked against anyone who wanted his land."

"But suppose someone knew he was thinking of selling the property to a developer, and a resort would be built on the island, or something like that, and they wanted to stop it." Emily leaned forward, her blue eyes eager.

"I haven't heard of any schemes like that, but I guess it's possible."

"There could be other people we don't know about who had something against him . . . People who don't live in Baxter."

"Yes." Nate shifted in his chair to face her. "But then why come all the way up here to do it? He was in his house in Gardiner up until a week before his death, and he lived alone. Why wait? I'd think it would be easier to get away with it down there, not up here where the community is so small, and every boat going out to the islands is noticed."

"Hmm." Emily shrugged. "But he — or she — got away with it. So far."

"It's early yet. Let the police do their job."

Emily sat back and studied her notepad. "I was thinking that on the next sunny day I'd take the boat over to the mainland and go to the town office to look up all the landowners out here."

"If we ever get another sunny day."

She grinned. "I just hope I get a few nice days to enjoy the lake this week. Was I stupid to pack my swimsuit?"

He laughed. "You know what they say about Maine weather."

"Yeah, two seasons. July and winter." Emily looked down at her pad. "Okay, so we have the grandchildren, the other island property owners, environmentalists, Vital Women, and the boys' camp. That's a pretty long list of people with a possible motive."

"Yeah. And any of them might have had the opportunity."

They sank into silence again. The firelight illuminated her face, and Nate watched her.

When she stirred, her blond hair glimmered. He wondered for the thousandth time if he had a chance with her.

The rain pelted the roof rhythmically, and Emily stretched and yawned. Nate looked at his watch and realized it was getting late.

"I'd probably better vamoose." He stood up.

"I wish you didn't have to go out in this weather," she said.

Nate knew it wasn't an invitation. He knew Emily better than that. Even after all these years, now that they were both twenty-five, with no parents looking over their shoulders, she wouldn't ask him to stay. Since her return, he'd seen that her faith was still important to her. That revived his old admiration for her. Emily had become a strikingly beautiful and successful woman, but her character hadn't changed. She was still a loyal friend and strong in her faith.

Nate realized he was staring down at her, mesmerized by her wistful face in the flickering firelight.

"The wind's died down a bit," he said. "I'll be fine."

Emily rose and brought his jacket from the sofa.

Before stepping out the door, he turned and looked at her. It was almost like high school . . . the dread moment of the good-bye. Her cheeks were still pink from the warmth of the fire, and her eyes shone as she smiled. He wondered if he could kiss her.

Nate hesitated. Seven years ago he'd dared to kiss her. Five seconds of bliss, then the most humiliating moment of his life, fol-lowed by months of agony and years of loneliness. It wasn't only her stepfather who caused that. Emily could have contacted him after she was out from under Brian Gillespie's roof, but she never did. No, kiss-ing Emily Gray was dangerous.

"Good night, Emily." He brushed her cheek with his knuckles, suppressing his longing, and opened the door.

7

When Emily awakened Tuesday morning, she wanted to scream. Rain still pattered lightly on the roof. Looking out the window, she saw that the path leading down to the wobbly dock was slick with mud.

Lord, she prayed silently as she dressed, *please help me not to let this weather get me down.*

A rainy day usually didn't bother her, but three in a row was her limit. She decided to defy the gray sky and donned shorts and a T-shirt, but even before she hit the top of the stairs, she knew she'd freeze and turned back to change into jeans and a maroon hoodie.

After breakfast, she ventured out and risked her neck on the muddy path to the dock. The rain was now a drizzle, and she became more hopeful when she spotted a lighter area in the sky to the south. A few boats were out, and two long war canoes put out from the boys' camp beach on Little Cat. Emily hugged herself and shivered. Maybe today was the day to go ashore and do research at the town office.

The thought of seeing Nate again warmed her. She realized she was thinking about him a lot these days. Last night had given her a lot to ponder.

They had drawn close during their brainstorming session before the fireplace. She'd felt an electric charge flowing between them, although they sat in separate chairs and didn't touch each other all evening. Nate felt it, too. She was sure he had.

She'd thought for a second, right before he left, that he was going to kiss her. When he backed off, her spirits had plunged from breathless anticipation to bleak disappointment. She'd wanted him to kiss her. She could admit that to herself and God. Seven years now, she'd waited for that kiss. And he'd wanted it, too.

What was holding him back? There wasn't another woman in his life, she was reasonably sure about that, judging from the conversations they'd had and the time he'd elected to spend with her over the last three days.

Was he still heeding Brian's ultimatum? That was ridiculous. Brian was dead, and his interference in their fledgling romance so long ago didn't matter now.

As she sat down on the dock and lowered herself into the aluminum boat, it struck her that Nate might feel inferior to her now. In childhood and adolescence, they were on an equal footing. They both came from families that scraped out a respectable living in a small town. They attended school together and were in the same classes until the last couple of years of high school. They competed more or less evenly for academic honors, though Nate excelled in mathematics while Emily thrived on language arts courses.

She climbed over the seats toward the stern of the boat, and the rainwater in the bottom of the boat seeped into her sneakers. She sat down on the middle seat with a sigh, picked up the coffee can that was standard equipment for islanders, and began to bail.

Was it the fact that she'd finished her education and he hadn't? But that was silly. Nate's family circumstances had caused him to terminate his education early. It wasn't his fault. And he was now a respected business owner in the community and seemed to be doing well running the marina his parents had built up over the years. That was nothing to be ashamed of.

But she couldn't help wondering if her return to Baxter had caused Nate to reevaluate his life. She had followed her plans to the letter — leave home as soon as possible . . . college in another state . . . summer jobs away from home . . . bachelor's degree in journalism . . . well-paying job at a large daily newspaper . . . bylined stories read by thousands every day.

Meanwhile, Nate was renting boats and delivering groceries.

She heard a motorboat and looked eagerly over the water. It wasn't Nate's cabin cruiser. She squinted, wishing she'd brought her binoculars. State troopers, she decided, as they veered toward Mr. Derbin's property. She made out two forms in the boat, wearing slickers and broad-brimmed hats.

Critically she surveyed the bottom of her boat. She couldn't get much more of the half inch of water out with the can. Moving to the stern, she pulled the cord on the motor.

Nothing.

She gritted her teeth and pulled again. A half-hearted whine, then nothing.

"Great."

She leaned back against the thwart and closed her eyes. She wouldn't believe that

Nate would let his pride keep him from renewing their friendship. Of course, a kiss meant much more than friendship. Maybe that was it. He didn't want to start a romance, knowing she'd leave in a few days. She'd left Baxter once and stayed away a long time. And she'd given him no hope to expect she'd return again after this visit.

"Hello, Emily!"

She opened her eyes and blinked. A ray of sun sneaked from beneath the clouds at the south end of the lake, yet fat drops of rain were splatting down into the boat and the lake around her.

Mr. Rowland was walking along the path between the cottages, with a prancing golden retriever on a leash.

"Have you been ashore?" he called.

"No. I was going to, but I can't start the motor."

Mr. Rowland stepped onto her dock and stopped as it swayed beneath his weight. "I'm not much good with outboards. Guess you'll have to get Nate to check it." He winked at her.

Emily nodded. The dog sniffed at the post where the boat was tied.

"I didn't know you had a dog."

Mr. Rowland grinned. "This is Tootie. I have to keep her penned up. Folks don't

121

like dogs loose out here, and Mr. Derbin made it clear he didn't want her running about on his property."

So, Emily thought, *even animals are forbidden to step on Derbin land.* She remembered her mother's frequent reminders when she was a girl. *Don't you go up there. Mr. Derbin tolerates us, but he likes his privacy.*

"Have you seen the new *Journal*?" Mr. Rowland asked.

"No. Is it out yet?"

"Bob Kimmel has a copy. He went into town this morning to make a phone call."

Emily scowled at her uncooperative motor. "Well, I guess I'm not going to get there today unless Nate drops by."

"Likely he will," said Mr. Rowland. "He always takes the mail to the boys' camp after lunch, and if anything comes for the folks here on Grand Cat, he'll deliver it. I suspect he'll stop by to say hi to a certain young lady."

Emily swallowed hard. Did everyone in town except Nate consider them a couple?

"We're old friends," she managed.

"Sure, I understand."

She stood and grasped the edge of the dock, and Mr. Rowland extended his hand to give her a lift.

"Thanks."

Tootie pulled on the leash, and Mr. Rowland tugged back. "Just a minute, girl." He focused on Emily again. "Bob says he'll give me his *Journal* after he and Angela read it. It's full of Felicia's stories about the murder. Of course, it's all stuff we heard over the weekend. And the interview with you, too. The photo's a good likeness."

"Thank you. Felicia wanted to announce my visit to the folks who used to know me and my family."

"Well, I can't wait to read the article."

He and Tootie walked with her to shore, and Emily held her breath as the dock shook.

"Felicia made quite a story about the identity of the murderer," Mr. Rowland went on. "She asked a lot of folks in Baxter who they thought did it."

She shrugged. "When you don't have facts about something like this, people still want to talk about it."

"I s'pose she needed to fill the space. Anyway, most people seem to agree that the murder had to have been done by someone on the island."

"That's nonsense."

"Maybe, and maybe not."

Emily looked down at her feet. Mud squelched up the sides of her sneakers.

"Really, Mr. Rowland, anyone could have come out in a boat on Saturday and killed Mr. Derbin."

"But none of the neighbors remembers seeing a boat land on the island, other than people who have cottages here and those going to the Vital Women Wilderness Retreat. Raven made a couple of trips to shore that morning in her red speedboat. And of course, people were coming and going from the boys' camp, but there's half a mile of water between us and them on Little Cat. The *Journal* says that if any strangers came to Grand Cat in a motorboat, the cottage residents would have noticed. All the people Felicia interviewed agree on it."

Emily shook her head. "I'm still not convinced."

She managed to extricate herself from the conversation, and Mr. Rowland and Tootie continued along the path that rounded the back of the cottages, toward Raven's retreat center.

Emily stepped out of her muddy sneakers on the porch and went inside. She picked up her useless cell phone from the counter. Her list of reasons for wanting to talk to Nate was growing. There was the outboard motor, of course, and that shaky dock. She ought to call her mother and secure permission for Nate to order a new dock. Those thoughts, added to her frustration at not being able to get to the town office, drove her to punch in the phone number for the Baxter Marina and wait with minuscule hope for results. To her delight, she heard the ringing tone. One, two . . .

"Baxter Marina."

"Nate!" She bounced on her toes, excited that she'd succeeded, and thrilled to hear him speak.

"Emily?"

"Yes. You sound like you've got your head in a bait bucket."

"What say?"

"I said — oh, never mind what I said. I want to talk to you."

Dead silence.

"Nate?"

She sighed and lowered the phone from her ear. The reception bars were nonexistent on the display.

She stamped her foot and laid the phone none too gently on the drain board. Isolation. That's what people came here for. Well, she was getting it in spades.

Suddenly she remembered Nate's words when they'd found the body. The high point of the island! She snatched up the phone and dashed onto the porch. The clouds were lifting. The surface of the lake was calmer than it had been in days. A few drops splattered down from the trees, but the rain had stopped.

She stuffed the phone in her pocket and struggled into her sneakers, smearing mud along her thumb, but she didn't bother to go in and wash. Instead, she wiped it on the knee of her jeans.

As she hurried outside and around to the back of her cottage, she planned her route. She couldn't go along the shore to the north. The marshy area where the herons nested would block her path that way. She crossed the trail that led behind the other cottages and struck off between the pines.

All I have to do is go uphill.

It was harder than she'd anticipated, wading through the unchecked undergrowth. She toiled on, the wet bushes and low limbs of evergreens soaking her pants as she brushed against them.

You're trespassing, a little voice said in her head.

Mr. Derbin's dead, she retorted. *He doesn't care anymore.*

The trees became thinner, and low, spreading shrubs took over. At last she reached a small clearing at the top of the slope. The spongy ground gave beneath her feet, and in places she could see where the heavy rain had eroded patches of topsoil.

At the highest point, she was able to see in all directions. Far to the northeast, she could see the majestic, snow-topped summit of Katahdin. She gulped and slowly turned a full circle. She was only a hundred feet or so above Blue Heron Lake, she supposed, but she had a view of the lake and Grand Cat that no one else had seen in years. She spotted the roof of Mr. Derbin's cabin below her, and in the other direction she could see the roof of a large building that she supposed was the lodge at the Vital Women center.

Closer, on the rocky west side of the island, the hill sheared away in a cliff. As she surveyed the expanse of unbroken forest on the shore beyond, a huge bird flew toward her, flapping its blue-gray wings, and glided in to land in a huge pine tree below Emily. The treetop swayed as the heron settled into the blotch that must be its nest of sticks high in the pine.

She pulled in a deep breath and turned around to face the town of Baxter, nearly a mile away across the lake. Fumbling in her pocket, she retrieved the cell phone.

"All right, you. Don't fail me now."

She punched in the numbers and held her breath.

"Hello."

"Nate?"

"Emily!"

"Yeah." The comfort of his voice washed over her.

"I can hear you this time."

"Guess where I am."

"In town?"

"No."

"You can't be on the island."

"I am."

"No, you're not."

"Wanna bet?"

After a brief pause, his said, "Don't tell me you're up on the roof."

She laughed. "The roof of the island, maybe. I'm on the hill."

"You're kidding. You went on Mr. . . ."

"Yes, I did."

"Wow."

She smiled at the awe in his voice. "Oh, come on, it doesn't matter anymore, does it?"

"I dunno. I mean, when I was a kid, my dad drilled it into me that nobody, but nobody, trespasses on Derbin land."

"Yeah, I got the same routine from my folks. But now . . ."

"What's it like?"

"It's fantastic. Nate, I can see Katahdin."

"Wow."

"And I can see your docks at the marina, too. Little Cat. Blue Spruce Island. I can almost see to Canada. Why didn't I bring my camera? Felicia would buy my exclusive photos for the *Journal*."

"You must have been really desperate to climb up there."

"I was."

"Are you all right?"

"Yes, I'm fine."

"What's so important, then?"

She swallowed hard. "Several things. I mean, the . . . the dock, and . . . and I couldn't start the boat motor, and . . ."

"Those don't sound urgent. I'll stop by later and take another look at that motor. Maybe some water got into the gas tank."

"Okay. I'll . . . look for you after lunch."

"Was there something else, Em?"

Her heart was pounding, all out of proportion to the circumstances. *It's because I hiked up here,* she told herself.

"I just . . . wanted to talk to you. I'm sorry, Nate. I know you're busy." Suddenly she felt childish. "Look, we'll talk later, all right? If you have a few minutes."

"Sure. I'll come by your place last, so we'll

129

have plenty of time. But you've got me curious now."

"Sorry."

"Just give me a hint. What's it about?"

She hesitated. How stupid would this sound? Was it worth endangering the new closeness they'd found? But even though he was glad to have her here, Nate was keeping an invisible barrier between them, no question about that. It might be easier to raise the subject when he wasn't looking at her with those huge brown eyes.

She gulped for air. "Okay, here's the deal. Is there something bothering you about our date?"

"Our . . . what? What date? You mean church last Sunday?"

"Nathan Pierce Holman! You know very well what I'm talking about. The one and only date we ever had!"

Silence again. Emily's stomach seemed to drop away.

Oh, no, oh no! Why did I say that? Now I've ruined everything.

"Actually, I've been thinking about it a lot."

She breathed. "You have?" It was a squeak, more than a question.

"Well, yeah, Em, I have. As a matter of fact, since you came back, I've hardly thought about anything else. I mean . . . that was one of the strangest things that ever happened to me."

"H–how do you mean, strange?"

"Well . . . let me ask you. When I kissed you that night . . ."

"Yeah?" Emily pushed the phone against her cheek to stop her hand from trembling.

"What did that mean to you?"

Her stomach fluttered as she inhaled. "You want the truth?"

"Nothing but."

"It was . . . a turning point in my life."

"Oh, come on, you're exaggerating."

"No." She found a lump suddenly obstructing her throat. "It was a very influential moment for me. That kiss . . ." She bit her lip.

"Yeah?" Nate whispered.

"It sort of became the standard."

"What kind of standard? You mean it was a standard kiss?"

"Hardly. It was . . . the standard by which I judged all the guys I dated after that."

"Oh, and that would be quite a few, I guess."

She winced. "Not so many. But I . . . I just couldn't seem to get close to a guy after . . . Aw, Nate, that night is the reason I haven't found the right man yet."

Scary dead silence.

"I'm not sure I heard you correctly, Em."

"Yes, you did."

"You're saying it's my fault you're single and lonely?"

"I didn't say that! You're putting words in my mouth."

"Yeah? Then what did you mean?"

She tugged at her hair and sighed. "This was a bad idea. Let's wait and talk about it when you come out this afternoon."

"I want to talk about it now." The phone crackled, and she wondered if he was clenching it, strangling her by proxy, or if they were about to lose their connection again.

She ground her teeth together. *What have I started? Lord, as usual, I've jumped in without considering the consequences. Now Nate's mad, and I'm going to have to do a lot of explaining. Help me out of this mess. Please!*

"Well, what exactly do you want to know?" she asked.

"How is this my fault? I mean, do I blame you for my life?"

"I don't know. Do you?"

"No," Nate said. "I like my life. Mostly."

"Okay. I'm glad."

She heard him sigh, and then his repentant

voice came. "I lied. I hate my life sometimes, and yes, I suppose some it has to do with . . . Tell me, Em, how did I keep you from finding the love of your life?"

"I guess by . . . giving me something to compare other people to. I mean, whenever I'd meet someone new and he seemed interested, I'd always compare him to you."

"But, you weren't comparing them to me," Nate protested. "You were comparing them to a memory, or maybe the memory of a fantasy, not the real me."

"Nate, I hate this. I made a big mistake in calling you. We ought to talk about this in person."

"You're right. I'll be there in two hours."

"O . . . kay." She nudged at a small speckled rock with the toe of her sneaker and eased it out of the soft earth. Suddenly another rock near it came into focus, and Emily froze. That was no rock. The elongated sections formed a pattern that she recognized with sickening clarity. It couldn't be, but it was. There was nothing else it could be. Protruding from the earth was a hand. A skeletal, human hand.

8

Nate jerked the phone away from his ear when Emily yelped. Cautiously, he put it back, his heart racing.

"Emily, what is it? What's wrong?" Unwelcome images flashed through his mind, of Emily alone on the isolated hilltop with Henry Derbin's murderer lurking in the shadows.

"It's . . ." Emily breathed deeply. "It's a skeleton, Nate."

"What? You're kidding!"

"No, I'm not kidding. At least, I can see a hand sticking out of the mud."

"A hand?" he whispered.

"Well . . . Those are definitely bones. They look like fingers to me." She gulped. "Nate, there've got to be more bones under the dirt."

He turned his back to the store, where several customers were browsing. "Okay, don't panic."

"What should I do?"

"Can you get to the Derbins' cabin from there?"

"Yeah, I think so. It'll be a steep climb down and there's no path, but I think it would be faster than if I go all the way down and around by the shore."

"All right, a couple of troopers took a boat out this morning. Go to Mr. Derbin's and see if they're still there. But be careful. Don't fall and hurt yourself."

"I won't."

"I'll call the police and be there as fast as I can." He paused. "You okay?"

"Yeah." Her voice was shaky.

Nate hated to let go of their only means of communication. "Just be careful. I'll be there soon."

"Thanks," said Emily.

He hung up the phone.

Emily was out there alone in the middle of the woods, trekking down a sodden hillside, probably scared stiff. No, not scared stiff. Emily was strong. But she had sounded frightened. He didn't blame her. If she was right about what she had just seen, then for the second time in less than a week, she'd discovered a dead body. He remembered how rattled he had been the first time. Emily must be shaken to the core. He had to get there fast, to be there for her.

"Excuse me."

He turned around. A middle-aged woman with dyed blond hair stood at the counter holding a jug of milk and a fistful of wrapped beef jerky strips. "For the kids," she said, in a heavy southern accent.

Nate tried to free enough of his mind to communicate. "Oh," he managed.

"Not like they didn't get enough to eat back at the Pancake Shack," the woman went on. "And those prices are outrageous." She set her things on the counter. "It's so hard to find anything they can eat in the car without making a mess. Do you have any string cheese?"

"Over there in the dairy case."

As she turned toward where he pointed, Nate rushed to the post office window. "Hey, Mom, I need you to cover the store."

"What's going on?"

She could always read his face. Nate glanced around. "I'll explain later, but it's important."

"Okay."

She closed the post office window. As she came through the doorway, Nate met her.

"Can I use the phone in there?"

"Of course."

She headed for the counter, where two

customers now waited for service. Nate entered her tiny post office cubicle and picked up the phone. To his relief, the police dispatcher answered almost at once.

"This is Nate Holman at the marina in Baxter. Do you have some officers on Grand Cat Island?"

"Let's see, Trooper Taylor checked in about an hour ago, but I'm not sure where he's at now."

"Well, I need an officer at Blue Heron Lake ASAP." Nate quickly explained the situation. "I'm heading out to the island now," he said. "The marina will have a boat ready for the officers if they need it."

He hung up the phone and dashed out the back door. When he reached the dock he saw that the boat they'd loaned the police that morning was back in its place, which meant there were no cops on Grand Cat.

He'd sent Emily on a pointless quest.

Emily put her phone back in her pocket. She started toward the tree line in the direction of Mr. Derbin's cottage without looking back. When she got a third of the way down the slope, the trees closed in thick around her, and last autumn's dead leaves rustled under her feet.

Just keep going down, she told herself.

She looked over her shoulder, back up the hill, and her sneakers slipped on the damp leaves. Scrambling to her feet, she pushed aside the underbrush that hindered her descent, but it was hard to see where to put her feet. She plunged forward, the momentum from each downward step carrying her farther than she'd expected.

All the while, her mind raced, making it hard to focus on footholds and handholds. The bony hand was seared into her memory. Was there an intact skeleton attached to it? How long since someone buried it there? And whose body lay on the hilltop?

She stopped to rest on a ledge of granite, panting as she held on to a spindly gray birch for support. The rugged hillside offered no easy way down. She wondered if anyone had ever hiked through these woods. Just the wildlife, she supposed. Squirrels and raccoons, and an occasional deer that swam out from the shore. Maybe Indians, a long time ago, and the big cats that supposedly gave the island its name.

When she had caught her breath, she started down again. Just as she spotted a patch of leafy berry bushes steaming in the sunlight near the bottom of the hill, her foot slipped on a patch of damp, orange pine needles, and she pitched forward, thrusting her hands out to break her fall.

Her breath whooshed out of her, and she lay on the wet ground for a moment before rolling over and taking stock of the damage. Her left shin burned from slamming against a stump. She wiped her wet hands on her jeans, wincing as she stood up. A small building with weather-beaten shingles for siding stood a few yards away.

She rushed toward it and around the side of the building. There didn't seem to be any windows, and the door was secured with a shiny steel padlock through a rusty hasp. A storage shed, she guessed. She turned away and saw a faint path through the trees. Limping along it, she saw with relief that the back of Mr. Derbin's cottage lay fifty feet in front of her.

Ignoring the pain in her shin, she ran to the cottage and pounded on the front door. "Hello! I need some help!"

In a few seconds, Andrew Derbin opened the inner door and came out onto the veranda.

"What's going on?"

"Are the police here?" Emily shifted her weight to ease the pain in her leg. "I need to talk to them."

Andrew shook his head. "They were here

earlier, but they left." He stared at her. "You're Emily."

"That's right." She swallowed hard.

"Nate Holman told me you were back in town."

"I'm sorry I bothered you." She realized she looked a sight, her jeans muddied, her face flushed, and her hair disheveled.

"Why do you need the cops?" Andrew's voice was wary. "Do you know something about my grandfather's death?"

"No." Emily backed down the steps, wanting at all cost to avoid an explanation. There was no sense in setting the island abuzz with more gossip.

"What do you need them for?" He shoved the porch door open and followed her outside.

"It's something else."

His stern voice and narrowed eyes sent a prickle up Emily's spine. She looked toward the water. A boat in the distance plowed through the waves, heading for the aluminum dock below them.

"There's Nate!" She ran down the path toward the dock.

She heard footsteps behind her and realized Andrew was following her.

"What's going on?" he yelled.

Emily ran out to the end of the dock.

When the boat was a few yards out and Nate cut the motor, she looked back over her shoulder. Andrew was still coming toward her.

As Nate reached the dock, Andrew stopped and stood at the far end.

Nate secured the boat and climbed out. Emily rushed to him, into the warmth of his arms.

"You okay?"

"Yes."

He held her close for a second. Emily hadn't realized how her body shook until she felt his sturdy arms embracing her. She tried to speak, but found her voice caught in her throat.

"What do you want?" Andrew strode toward them.

Nate dropped his arms, but grasped Emily's hand in his. "I came out to get Emily."

Andrew crossed his arms. He and Nate stared at each other for a long moment.

"She said she needed the police." Andrew eyed Emily with a frown.

"It's all right." Nate's voice was smooth and steady. Emily wished she had his composure. "I was talking to the dispatcher a few minutes ago, and they have someone coming out to see Emily. I'm going to take her to the marina to meet them."

Andrew stood still for another moment. "This doesn't have to do with Grandpa?"

"No." Nate squeezed Emily's hand.

"Then why did you come here?"

She pulled in a deep breath. "I'm really sorry if I upset you, Andrew. I thought the state troopers would be here."

"Yeah, well, they were out here a while ago to bring me Grandpa's personal effects, but they didn't stay long."

He turned back toward the cottage, his shoulders slumped.

"The police should arrive at the marina soon," Nate said softly. "We'll go meet them there. You'll probably have to come back out to the island with them, though, to show them what you found."

She nodded, and he climbed down into the boat, then helped her in.

"I'm so sorry this happened to you, Em."

"It's okay. I just . . . wish you'd been with me."

"Well, I'm here now." He handed her a life jacket.

"Will you come with us? When I show them, I mean?"

"Absolutely."

She smiled then, although her lips quivered as she fastened the straps on the life preserver with clumsy fingers. Nate didn't qualify his response with "if the troopers let me." He was willing to be leaned on. All right, she would lean.

He shoved the boat away from Andrew's dock and started the engine. Emily sat down, taking deep breaths and uttering a silent prayer. She fell back into a habit she'd developed while working on stressful assignments. While on the way back to her desk at the newspaper office, she would always put the event she was covering in perspective and begin mentally composing her article.

She stared out over the rough surface of the lake.

Human remains were discovered Tuesday on Grand Cat Island in Blue Heron Lake. The investigating officer said the unidentified body was recovered and taken to the state crime lab in Augusta. The bones were buried in a shallow grave near the island's highest point, and were apparently revealed by erosion during the recent heavy rains. A cottage owner found the grave site while hiking . . .

How would Felicia write it, she wondered. Certainly the story on page one of next week's *Journal* would not be as direct and dry. She could almost see the headlines. TERROR GRIPS ISLAND RESIDENTS. BONES FOUND ON FORBIDDEN LAND.

She jumped as Nate touched her hair. She

looked over at him, and he let his hand rest on her head for a moment, then bent and reached for her hand and squeezed it. She squeezed back and didn't let go.

9

Emily and Nate went to the hilltop with the police officers Tuesday evening. She pointed out the discolored phalanges and carpal bones lying in their distinctive array. When they came down the hillside at dusk, the Kimmel boys saw them. On Wednesday morning, there was no keeping the island dwellers away from the investigation.

Gossip ripped the length of Grand Cat over propane grills and waterskiing floats. When no fewer than eight officers and crime scene investigators arrived after breakfast, the neighbors would not be excluded.

Detective Blakeney detailed Gary to string yellow plastic tape from slender stakes in a broad circle around the location of the body to keep the people at a distance.

That a body did indeed lie beneath the soil had been determined the evening before, with the help of powerful spotlights and gentle probing.

Now the excavation began in earnest.

Nate went early to Emily's cottage, and they made the trek once more with Blakeney and the rest of the police contingent. Emily brought a quilt, and they spread it on the ground just outside the yellow circle.

The Kimmels, all three boys and their cheerfully confident parents, appeared next, then a cluster of tanned women from the Vital Women Wilderness Retreat. Jenna came over and spoke to Emily politely, then turned her eyes on Nate.

"So, you're out early today, Mr. Postman."

Nate smiled. "So are you."

"Gotta be where the action is."

She watched him as though waiting for something. An invitation to sit on the blanket, maybe? Nate glanced at Emily. Her face held a studious look of indifference, and he realized suddenly that she was wondering how well he knew Jenna.

"Isn't it great to have sun again?" Jenna unzipped her sweatshirt and Nate looked away as she pulled it off and tied it around her waist. Her orange tank top left little to the imagination.

He reached for Emily's hand, and she smiled at him and squeezed his fingers. Good old Em! He'd missed her so much. Right now he hoped she could read his mind and knew she was the only one who had a chance with his heart.

He glanced briefly up at Jenna. "Yeah, it's great."

Truly Vigue came next, with Marvin puffing along behind her. Another couple soon arrived; the Wilcoxes, who had the cottage between the Vigues and the Kimmels. Their two children were older than he and Emily. "Grown and gone," Mrs. Wilcox would lament when Nate handed her the mail, which frequently included postcards from their flight attendant daughter, Tracie.

Felicia Chadwick strode into the clearing, marched straight to the yellow tape boundary, and began focusing her camera on the investigators inside the circle.

"Well, the press is here," Emily said.

"Part of it." Nate nodded toward the newly formed path the islanders had followed up from the cottage area. Two young men, one of them carrying a video camera, approached the summit. Behind them came Rocky Vigue, panting and pausing every few steps for breath.

"I can't believe Rocky made it all the way up here," Emily murmured.

"Yeah," Nate said.

"I wonder how the TV crew heard about this."

"It was all over town last night. I think Marvin went ashore and spread the word before I left your place."

Truly walked over and plopped down beside Emily without asking permission. "You kids were smart to bring a blanket."

Emily said nothing, but gave her a tight smile.

"Hey there, Nate and Emily," Marvin boomed. "Terrible thing! Terrible thing."

"I'm almost glad Henry Derbin didn't live to see this day," Truly said, shaking her head. "All these people traipsing all over his land, when he didn't want anyone up here."

Yeah, all these people, Nate thought. He winked at Emily. But so far Andrew hadn't protested the convergence of the people on his land.

Jenna's upper lip curled. "I heard the old fellow didn't want anyone up here. Well, maybe he had a reason. Ever think of that?"

Emily's blue eyes widened, and she threw Nate a look of repulsion.

He stroked her hand and leaned toward her. "Want to go down?"

"Do you think the police want us to stay here?"

"I don't see why they would. I can tell Gary we'll be at your place."

She hesitated. Movement on the other

side of the small crowd caught Nate's eye, and he saw Andrew coming up the steeper slope from his grandfather's cottage, the way Emily had stumbled down the hill last night. He stopped a few yards from the others and stood with his hands in his pockets, watching the officers.

"What do you suppose is going through his mind?" Truly pulled off her sunglasses and stared at Andrew.

Nate cleared his throat. "This has got to be a shock for him."

"Yes, and he just lost his old grandpa," Marvin agreed. "Poor boy."

"He's not a boy," Truly said. "He's Rocky's age. Last time I checked, thirty-year-olds were not boys."

"Here come some more of our guests." Jenna walked away, toward a handful of women coming up the slope.

"I guess the ladies' retreat has no end of entertainment for their paying company this week," Marvin said, watching Jenna's retreating figure.

Truly scowled at him, and Nate guessed she thought Marvin was observing with a little too much interest.

Another woman joined them, and Truly leaned over and touched Emily's forearm.

"Do you know Angela Kimmel, dear?"

"Uh, no." Emily started to rise, but Angela knelt on the edge of the quilt.

"Don't get up. Hi, it's nice to meet you." She stuck her hand out, and Emily shook it. "Emily Gray."

"Isn't this the limit? I thought my boys were making it up when they told us last night another body'd been found."

"Unfortunately, it's true," Nate said.

Angela nodded. "They're so excited. Riley thinks it must be an old Indian burial site."

"Oh, I don't think so," Truly said.

"Why not?"

"Could be." Marvin nodded. "Yes, I suppose it could be."

"There might be other bones buried all around here."

Angela shivered, smiling. "Just think! We could be in the middle of an ancient grave-yard."

"Maybe that's why Mr. Derbin didn't want anyone up here," Marvin said. "If he knew it was sacred ground, why then —"

"Mr. Derbin wasn't religious," Truly cut in, "and he certainly wasn't a Native American."

A boy charged between the grown-ups and skidded to his knees beside Angela.

"Hey, Mom, did you hear? Somebody over there said it's Mrs. Derbin's bones."

"Mrs. —" Angela looked rather green at that moment.

"That's impossible," Marvin said, shaking his head.

"Yes," Truly said. "Nancy Derbin is buried in the village cemetery. Marvin and I attended the service."

"But did you actually see the body?" The boy's eyes were round, and his face melded into a mask of ghoulish delight. "Wa-ha-ha!"

"Stop it, Jet." Angela swatted his shoulder.

Truly aimed her annoyed expression at the boy. "I assure you, those bones over there are not Mrs. Derbin's. It's very naughty to spread rumors."

The boy's rubbery face became a mocking grimace.

"Jet," Angela said softly.

He jumped up and ran to join his father and brothers a few yards away.

"Kids." Angela shrugged.

Truly arched her eyebrows, but said nothing.

Nate glanced at Andrew again. He seemed to wilt, growing smaller in the bright sunlight. Leaning toward Emily, Nate whispered, "Do you mind if I go speak to Andrew for a second?"

"Not if you don't mind if I tag along."

Nate smiled and got up, pulling on her hand as she rose.

"Excuse us for a minute," Emily said, smiling at Marvin, Truly, and Angela.

Andrew didn't look away from the investigators until Nate and Emily were three feet from him. Then his gaze swerved their way for an instant and back again to the diggers.

"Hey, Nate. Emily."

"Hello, Andrew," Nate said. "I guess the police notified you last night."

He nodded. "Pretty weird."

Emily cleared her throat. "I wanted to tell you . . ."

Andrew pivoted and faced them. "This is what you were so shook up about yesterday, isn't it?"

She nodded and gave a miserable sigh. "I'm sorry, Andrew. It was an accident that I discovered this, and . . . well, I shouldn't have been up here. I'm sorry I came on your property without asking you. That was wrong of me. I wanted to see if my cell phone would work up here, and I guess I rationalized that with your grandfather dead, no one would care. But I still should have . . ." She let it trail off and squeezed her lips together.

"Hey, it's done," Andrew said. He took a pair of reflective sunglasses from his pocket and slipped them on. "It's probably a good thing, Emily. I mean, if you hadn't come up here, no one ever would have known about this."

Emily swallowed and looked up at Nate with big, mournful eyes.

"Thanks for understanding," Nate said to Andrew. "Yesterday when I came to your place, I wasn't sure what Emily had found, so we figured we'd better keep it quiet until the police came."

"Sure, sure." Andrew shook his head a little and seemed to be staring at the excavators again. "It's like some kind of archaeology dig, you know?"

"Maybe that's what it will turn out to be," Nate said.

Andrew sighed. "If it's some Indian thing, then the tribes will want the island for a holy place."

Nate darted a look at Emily. One more thing to add to her list of people who wanted this land, maybe.

"Do you think it's a very old site?" Emily asked.

"How should I know? I haven't been up here since I was a kid." Andrew's jaw worked back and forth for a moment. "I don't know why this is happening." He turned suddenly to Nate. "You think this is

153

another murder? I mean, Grandpa . . . now this . . ."

"Well . . ." Nate looked at Emily, but she just fumbled for his hand. "We don't know. But the bones . . . the hand bones, I mean . . ."

"Yeah?" Andrew's jaw stuck out toward him, and Nate looked straight at his own reflection in the sunglasses, trying to imagine the cool blue eyes behind them.

"Well, there wasn't any . . ." Nate hesitated.

"There's no skin or anything," Emily said quietly. "This body's been here awhile."

Andrew was still for a few seconds, then turned back toward the police line. His shoulders drooped once more.

Two investigators were kneeling in the dirt, and three other officers stood around them. The two on the ground were using tools and brushes to remove the sodden earth bit by bit.

"Funny how you came back and started poking around finding dead bodies," Andrew said.

Nate stared at him, scarcely believing what he'd heard. Emily's face had gone a stark white.

"I . . . didn't intend it that way." Something akin to panic now lit her eyes.

154

"She was with me Saturday, Andrew," Nate said. "Your grandfather had asked me to take him a few groceries. I would have done it whether Emily was here or not."

"And I didn't come up here yesterday to poke around," she said. "I wanted to talk to Nate, and my phone wouldn't work down at the cottage. I know I shouldn't have . . ."

She stopped, and Nate gave her hand a squeeze.

"I didn't mean anything," Andrew said, not looking at them. "It's funny, that's all. And that Chadwick woman will come pester me about it."

"You don't have to talk to her," Emily said.

Andrew stood motionless.

"Well, I'm going to take Emily home," Nate said after a moment. "The police don't need us here."

"Yeah. I might as well go home, too." Andrew looked around at the small crowd, which seemed to have increased.

"There's Raven." Emily nodded to the far end of the gathering, beyond the Wilcoxes and the Kimmels. Raven Miller was flanked by several women of varying ages. All of them were chatting as they watched the police officers.

"Hey, man." Rocky shuffled in between Nate and Andrew and grasped Andrew's hand. "Creepy, huh?"

"You said it."

Nate nodded to the two men and eased Emily away. As they walked back toward where they'd been sitting earlier, he realized Emily's quilt had been appropriated by more neighbors.

"You want me to get the quilt?" he asked.

Emily shook her head. "Leave it."

Nate stopped beside Truly Vigue and touched her shoulder.

Truly looked up at him eagerly. "You talked to Andrew!"

"Yes."

"What did he say?"

"Not much. Truly, we're going down. Could you and Marvin bring Emily's quilt when you come, and drop it off at her place?"

"Sure. But you're leaving before the most exciting part!"

"What's that?" Nate asked.

"When they remove the body, of course!"

Angela Kimmel leaned in. "There could be clothes or buttons or . . . well, lots of things that would give a clue to the identity of the deceased."

Mrs. Wilcox, now ensconced on the blanket, stared past him.

"You're Emily Gray, aren't you?"

"Yes," Emily said.

"Welcome back, dear. I heard you're responsible for this gathering."

Emily stiffened and threw Nate a helpless look.

"Word gets around," he said with a smile.

"Well, I think it's good that you found this . . . whatever it is," Mrs. Wilcox said. "I mean, here we've had a murder on the island a few days ago, and now we find there's another corpse. There could be a serial killer right here on Grand Cat! I said to Ed that we ought to pack up and go away for a week or two, until the police find out who's doing this. I mean, we could all be in danger if we stay here!"

"Do you really think so?" Marvin asked. He had sat down on the edge of the quilt, too, and appeared to be quite comfortable.

Truly frowned. "Well, nobody lives out here all winter, and we were the first to open our cottage this year."

Marvin nodded. "We got here in May, before Memorial Day."

"We were even here before Raven this year," Truly confirmed.

"And then Raven opened her place for guests a week or two ago," Marvin went on. "Then the Rowlands and Henry Derbin came, then . . ."

"What does it matter who came when?" asked Angela Kimmel, one of the latecomers.

"Well, I'm just saying, these killings didn't start until most everyone had their cottage open for the season."

"These killings?" Angela shook her head. "You think this body here has something to do with Mr. Derbin's murder?"

"Well, we don't know, do we?" Marvin asked.

"That's right," said Mrs. Wilcox.

Emily's face held dismay now.

Nate held up his hand and chuckled. "Listen, nobody's missing, right?"

The neighbors sat for a moment, digesting that.

"Oh, right, right," Marvin said with a chuckle. "At least, not that we know of. We don't know all of the ladies who come to the Wilderness Retreat."

Truly blinked rapidly and frowned at Nate. "You're saying that this grave Emily found isn't fresh, is that it? Because no one who lives nearby is missing?"

Nate shrugged. "I'm speculating."

"As we all are," Marvin said heartily. Several other people, including the TV news reporter, Rocky, and Bob Kimmel, seemed to be attracted to his loud voice and drifted toward the quilt. "But there's something to that. Nate, boy, you're right."

"There was that lost hunter a few years back," Rocky said.

Nate gave Rocky a grudging nod as the memory surfaced. "You're right."

"Did they ever find him?" Angela asked.

"No." Marvin cocked his head to one side, gazing toward the excavation site. "It was the year before you bought your cottage, I think."

Bob Kimmel nodded. "We heard about it when we first came. That would make it four years ago, I guess."

"While you were away, Emily." Truly's smile was that of one in the know, her favorite position when news was being discussed.

"Other than that," Marvin said, "no one's gone missing around Baxter for . . . what? Ten years or more?"

"Twelve."

Everyone turned and stared at Raven.

She had moved in closer, along with Jenna and several other women. She grimaced and said between her teeth, "The last person I know about who disappeared here was Josh Slate. It was twelve years ago this week."

She turned and stalked toward the path, her long, dark hair swaying.

Jenna hastened to catch up with her, and the other Vital Women followed.

Nate looked down at Emily.

"Let's go," she whispered.

10

As Nate and Emily stepped onto her rickety dock, she relished the warm sun beating down on her shoulders. Finally, it felt like June, and the grim scene on the hilltop lost some of its ugliness.

"Let me take a look at that motor for you." Nate sat on the edge of the dock and eased his weight down into her boat, then gave the cord a quick tug. The engine roared into life.

Emily crossed her arms. "Why wouldn't it start for me?" she shouted, a little irritated.

Nate laughed. "It probably would have if you'd tried one more time." He let it run for a few seconds, then shut it off and climbed up beside her once more. Emily quelled her annoyance, realizing her worries about the murder and the discovery of the bones affected her attitudes about other things.

"Hey, when I go back, why don't I call

your mom about getting a new dock?" He took her hand and headed for firm ground.

"I'd really appreciate that." She hesitated, wondering if he was still thinking about yesterday's phone call from her. She didn't really want to talk about the past right now. Her and Nate's past, that was. Joshua Slate's past was another story. "Do you want to stay for lunch?"

He smiled. "Sure."

"I'll throw something together."

They went inside, and Nate set the table with paper plates while Emily pulled out a bag of chips and sandwich fixings. As she worked, she mulled over the speculations and rumors about the body. She could still hear Raven Miller's voice ringing in her mind. *Twelve years ago.*

Emily remembered Josh Slate's disappearance vividly, though she'd been only thirteen at the time. She turned to Nate. "Do you think that body was Josh Slate?"

Nate ripped two paper towels off the roll by the sink. "I don't know. He drowned. Didn't he?"

"That's what everyone assumed. They never found his body."

"It was so long ago." Nate carefully folded the paper towels in half and laid one beside each plate.

Emily dipped her knife in the mayonnaise jar. "I remember my mom covering the story. Rocky Vigue threw a party here on the island the night Josh disappeared, remember?"

"Yeah, and there were a lot of kids from Rocky's class at that party," said Nate. "Like Andrew Derbin and Raven Miller."

"And Raven was dating Josh Slate. She went white as a sheet this morning when you and Marvin started talking about missing people." Emily brought the sandwiches to the table. "Do you want to eat outside? It's so warm out."

"Good thinking. I'll get some lawn chairs from the porch."

Nate set up the chairs in the sun on the level ground down near the dock, and Emily carried their plates out. Nate asked the blessing, but she found she couldn't contain her curiosity long enough to eat.

"What if that is his body?"

"Well, I guess it's possible." Nate paused with a pickle slice halfway from the plate to his mouth.

"That would mean someone buried him the night of that party. Whoever it was didn't want his body found."

"It would put a whole new light on it," Nate agreed. He popped the pickle into his mouth and chewed thoughtfully. "I remember the guys talking about the party after. All summer, people would talk about it at the store."

"Yeah," Emily said. "The girls who went to the party wouldn't talk about it to kids my age, but the town was talking about nothing else."

Nate inhaled slowly. "They said Rocky's parents didn't know anything about it. They hadn't moved to their cottage for the summer yet. A bunch of kids came out here to party and had a pretty wild time of it. But I doubt anyone else would ever have known about it, except that Josh Slate never went home that night."

Emily thought for a moment. "Maybe I should go back to shore when you go, so I can call Mom and ask her about it. She was publishing the *Journal* back then, and she covered the story of his disappearance. I think she wrote several articles about Josh."

Reporting on that story had been very stressful for her mother, Emily remembered. Families didn't want it known that their children were at the party, and people were rude to Carol Gray when she asked them for information. Kids said mean things to Emily at school, demanding that she tell her mother to quit writing bad things in the paper. Carol printed the stories about Josh's disappearance, the party, and the illegal liquor and drugs that played a role that night. She even wrote an article about the memorial service Josh's family held a month later, and another saying the state police had closed the case, designating the death accidental.

Nate sat motionless, his eyes focusing somewhere in the distance. "I remember the next day. It was a Sunday. My dad didn't go to church with us. He went out with the other men to search for Josh."

"Didn't they find his boat that day?"

"Yeah. Dad and Jim Swallow found it drifting, way down below Blue Spruce Island."

"That's more than a mile down the lake."

Nate nodded. "Josh's life jacket was in the boat. After that, Dad chewed me out a hundred times, telling me to always wear my life vest, even if I was only going to be on the water a minute."

"They had divers out there, didn't they?" Emily stared at the expanse of water between the island and Baxter.

"Yeah, but after two or three days, they gave up."

"It could be that lost hunter's body, I suppose." Doubts immediately filled Emily's mind. Deer were seldom seen on the island. "Would a deer hunter come out here? And if there was a hunting accident, who buried him?"

Nate shook his head. "Seems unlikely."

They finished their sandwiches then took Nate's boat to the marina. Connie was inundated with customers and had called on Allison Woods to come in and tend the cash register for her. Local people had heard about the new discovery on Grand Cat and wanted news. Several new teams of journalists had arrived, hoping to rent a boat.

"Oh, good," Connie called as Nate and Emily came through the back door. "I haven't even had time to sort the mail yet."

"I'll take care of the boat rentals, Mom," Nate said. "Do you mind if Emily goes over to the house and uses the phone? She needs to call her mother, and it's too hectic here."

"Sure," Connie said with a weary smile. "Make yourself at home, Emily."

Nate was still busy when she'd made the call, and Emily walked the quarter mile to the town office and asked the clerk to help her find the property maps for Grand Cat. Half an hour later, she strolled back to the marina and found Nate filling out a form for a boat he was renting to a trio of people Emily instantly pegged as television journalists. The woman's makeup was camera perfect, and the two men accompanying her were laden with equipment bags.

"I can run you out to the island and show you how to get up there," Nate was saying, "but I'm warning you, it's a pretty rugged climb. There's not a proper trail." He eyed the woman's strappy slingbacks.

"Great," she muttered. "Well, we've got to go where the news is."

"They sell sneakers here," Emily said. The woman cleared her throat, ignoring the comment.

"My mom and Allison say they can handle things here, so let's go," Nate said.

Emily walked with him, ahead of the television crew, to the dock. She climbed easily into the boat and watched as the woman with the medium-heeled sandals stepped precariously off the dock, grabbing on to Emily's shoulder as she landed somewhat off balance in the boat.

"Sorry," she said.

"It's all right." Emily smiled, thinking of what the woman had ahead of her.

When they reached the island, Nate tied up at Emily's dock and helped the reporter and her camera crew disembark. He walked with them toward the path behind the cottages.

"See that gap in the trees over there? That's where people have been going up the hill. You just keep climbing until you reach the top."

Emily said nothing, but watched skeptically as the woman threw back her shoulders and approached the faint trail. The sun was tucking behind the clouds, and the temperature was dropping again. When she and Nate got inside the cottage, Emily put a kettle of water on the stove for hot chocolate.

"I'd forgotten how cold it can be here, even in summer." She pulled out the notepad she'd carried with her to shore.

"Well, it's not officially summer yet for a couple of days," Nate said with a smile. "But, yeah, we're three hundred miles or so north of where you've been living. It probably makes quite a difference."

Emily chuckled as they settled down in the living room.

"Mom had a lot of information about the party," she said. "Names, facts. She got out her files and read me some of the articles over the phone. I'm going to try to check Felicia's back files, and if I can't find copies, Mom will fax them to the *Journal* office."

"Good," said Nate.

"Are you sure it doesn't bother you if I do this?"

He shook his head. "We're in the middle of it now. It makes sense for us to work on it. I mean, we know everyone around here, and you need to sell your mom's property. The outcome could affect that." He smiled and gave a half shrug. "I'd like to work with you, if you don't mind."

A calm satisfaction flowed over Emily. If there was one thing she didn't want, it was conflict with Nate, and his mind would be an asset in her investigating. "Josh's body was never recovered. You knew that." She referred to the notes she'd taken while talking to her mother. "We were right about the divers. And they dragged the lake between Grand Cat and Baxter, but they were limited in how much they could do with their equipment."

"It's pretty deep."

"Right. Rocky and his guests were the last ones to see Josh alive. All of them were shocked when they heard he'd drowned. My mom said Rocky was devastated. She didn't even try to interview him. She did try to talk to his parents, but Truly blew her off and screamed at her. Marvin just said they had no idea the kids were going out to the cottage."

"Did she talk to any of the kids then?"

"A few, but most of the parents didn't want her talking to them. You know, I think those teenagers were scared. That's how it came out about the party. Rocky wasn't going to admit it, but some of them were so remorseful they told their parents and the police about it."

"Girls?"

"Especially the girls. They told the cops how Rocky got a keg of beer somehow and brought it out to the island."

"He must have had someone older get it for him."

"Good point. And someone brought pot, though no one admitted to knowing who. All of them were high by midnight, and nobody recalled actually seeing Josh leave."

Nate leaned in closer. "So we've got a remote island at midnight with a bunch of drugged-up teenagers. Anything can happen."

"That's what I was thinking," said Emily. "But there's more. Raven was Josh's girlfriend at the time. She said they'd had an argument, and Josh was angry. They took a walk down the shore, and he left her there, telling her to ride home with someone else. She showed the police where she'd last seen him, and no one could remember seeing him after that. But the kids all thought Josh left in a huff. No one started looking for him until the next day."

Nate leaned back in his chair and perused the ceiling. "You know, several people connected to the party are still tied to the island in one way or another. Rocky's parents still own a cottage. Andrew Derbin lives in Augusta, but he's come up here at least once every summer, to spend a week or two on the island with his grandfather. His sister, Pauline, too. Was she at the party?"

"No, she wasn't," said Emily. "She's a couple of years older than Andrew and had already graduated, I think. She probably wasn't invited."

"Are you sure? Rocky Vigue used to have a thing for her."

"That's right."

"Yeah, but Pauli was too sophisticated to look twice at him, so you're probably right. She wouldn't take him up on an invitation to a kegger, even if he asked her."

Emily nodded. A heavyset boy two years her junior would not be Pauli's type.

"I haven't seen her around Baxter for years, though," Nate said. "After Mrs. Derbin died, Andrew kept coming in the summer, but not Pauli."

"Interesting. And then there's Raven," said

Emily. Her mind drifted back again to the talk on the hill. "I wonder if she knew more than she told the police. She and Josh had dated for two years, or so the *Journal* said. They had to be pretty close, even though they were fighting at the time of the party."

"Oh, I'd imagine all of those kids knew more than they told," Nate said. "Of course, even what they did say might be suspect, considering the condition they were all in when it happened."

"True." Emily glanced down at her notepad. "Mom also mentioned Gretchen Langdon and Jonathan Woods. Are either of them still around Baxter?"

"Yep, Gretchen and her husband run the campground on the shore north of town. She's doing a good business this week, and it will be steady all summer. And Jonathan Woods still lives in town. He runs the service station. His wife, Allison, is the lady helping my mom at the marina today."

"That's right," Emily said. "But neither of them owns land out here on the island."

"I don't think so."

She tapped her pad. "A lot of those partying kids still have connections here. Another one, Rand Pooler. He's director of the boys' camp on Little Cat, isn't he?"

Nate nodded. "Yeah. Was he at the party?"

"He was on the list Mom dredged up for me." The teakettle whistled, and Emily stood up to get the hot chocolate.

There was a moment of silence when she'd handed him a warm ceramic mug and sat down again. She felt his eyes on her. Somehow she knew what he was thinking. Even after their busy day and discussion about the murder, she hadn't been able to fully push it from her own mind either.

"So," he said, "are you ready to talk about your phone call from the hill yesterday?"

11

Emily drew back into her armchair and pulled the afghan off the back, down over her shoulders. She picked up her ironstone mug and peered into it.

"You probably ought to get back to the marina," she said, not looking at Nate. "Your mother and Allison could use your help, I'm sure."

A smile flickered over Nate's face, and she thought again how handsome he had become in manhood.

"I'm sure they'll be fine for a few more minutes."

"Really? Because there were a lot of people in the store an hour ago."

"So, I'm welcome when I want to do sleuthing with you, but as soon as things get personal, you want me to leave."

She squirmed and kicked her sneakers off without untying them, then pulled her feet up under her in the chair.

"Come on, Emily."

"What?"

"You were always open with me. We're still friends. Don't put a padlock on your emotions now."

Padlock. A sudden image flashed through her mind of a shiny steel lock hanging from a rusty hasp.

"Nate, I saw an old lock —"

"Uh-uh. You're not changing the subject on me. You said you wanted to talk about that night seven years ago. Now's the time."

She felt her cheeks simmer. "All right, I admit I've avoided the subject. We both have."

"True, but . . . our time is running out. You'll only be here a few more days." His voice dropped to a deep undertone, and he reached over and gently pried her fingers off the edge of the afghan. "I don't want you to leave without knowing where I stand with you. Talk to me, Em. Please."

She closed her eyes for a moment and tried to imagine a future that included Nate. If it included Nate, then it would also have to include Baxter and Blue Heron Lake. She acknowledged inwardly that she liked that potential future, in spite of all the obstacles that would have to be overcome.

"All right."

His eyes were riveted on her, as though his life depended on her next few words. She swallowed down the anxiety in her throat.

"To me, that night . . . the night we went bowling in Aswontee . . ." She straightened her shoulders and looked him in the eye. "When you asked me . . ."

"After graduation," he prompted.

"Yes. I was thrilled. I'd hoped for so long that . . . that you would see me that way."

He squeezed her hand. "I guess it took me a while to get down to brass tacks."

She shrugged. "I didn't mind, not then. All that mattered was that you'd finally asked me out. Me. Not some other girl." She pressed her lips together and stared into the fireplace. "And when we came back and you kissed me . . . At that point, it became even more significant. I was having a rotten time that year, with Brian acting weird and Mom stressed out over him making her sell the paper and move away."

"I didn't know he made her."

"Yeah." She felt the tears coming and squeezed her eyes shut, but one escaped anyway, and she brushed it away with her sleeve. "Even though you were my best friend, there were things I didn't tell you."

"I'm sorry."

She nodded. "It's okay. Maybe it would have been better if I'd told you everything, I don't know. Anyhow, that date was very important to me. But obviously, it didn't mean as much to you."

"How can you say that?" Nate whispered. "Of course it meant a lot to me. It was the best day of my life . . . up until Brian made his entrance and ruined everything."

"Yeah?"

"Yeah."

She pulled her hand away. "Then why didn't you try to contact me after?"

"You went away a few days later, Em. What was I supposed to do?"

"I don't know. Come out to the island and see me before I left, maybe? Or ask my mom for my address and write me a letter?"

He sighed. "I'm so sorry, Emily. I did think of doing those things, but . . . well, to be honest, I was afraid to contact you for the next few days. Brian made such a big deal of it when he caught me kissing you."

"Scared you pretty good, huh?"

"Well, yeah."

She could see that he was uncomfortable even talking about it.

"I figured."

Nate laced his fingers together and studied his hands. "He made it clear that he didn't

177

want me coming around you."

"So you didn't."

He pulled in a deep breath and turned to face her. "I actually thought about coming out here during the day, while Brian was at the paper mill. But I knew someone would tell him. I didn't want to risk that."

"You were that scared?"

"I was terrified of him. But it wasn't just for me, Em. I thought . . . well, I was afraid he might . . . do something to you. You or your mom, even. I didn't want to make him mad again."

She felt the old dread creep over her as she watched the embers burn down. "I was scared, too. He had an awful temper."

"I know you were miserable after he married your mom. Did he ever hurt you, Emily?"

"No. Not physically. I think . . . I would have told you."

He captured her hand once more. "I hope so, Em. I worried about you. I could tell you weren't confiding in me like you used to when we were kids. I was glad in a way when you left home. I missed you terribly, but . . . I used to tell myself you were safe then."

"He never hit me or anything."

"I'm glad."

She inhaled sharply as another memory caught her unaware. She was fourteen, and six months after marrying Brian, her mother had stayed late at the *Journal* office to put together a new front page after some late-breaking news came in. Emily remembered her uneasiness, being at home alone with her stepfather that evening. He'd cajoled her into watching a movie together, but then had sat down near her on the couch, too close for comfort. She'd moved away, but Brian seemed to follow. *Hey, I'm your old man now,* he'd said, slipping his arm around her shoulders and leaning close. She'd wanted to gag. She excused herself and went to her room early. She heard him moving about downstairs, opening the refrigerator and walking about the living room and kitchen. Then the television went silent. She lay still in her bed, not breathing, listening. She heard the stairs creak, as though someone was mounting them stealthily.

Did I lock the door? She always locked her door now, but suddenly she began to shake. *What if I forgot?* She made herself lie still. He stopped outside her door, she was certain. Peering through the darkness, she stared toward the pristine white panels of the door.

The knob turned.

She almost screamed, but the door did not open. *So, I didn't forget. Thank you, God.*

As the quiet footsteps moved away, she heard another sound; tires crunching on the gravel driveway. Mom was home. Emily stayed in her bed, tears bathing her face. Fifteen minutes later, her mother came and knocked quietly on her door.

"Em, you awake?"

She'd bounded out of bed and thrown the lock, catapulting into her mother's arms.

"I'm so glad you're back!"

"Honey, what's wrong? Brian said you went to bed early. Aren't you feeling well?"

Emily drew her mother into her room, closed the door, and related to her in a breathless whisper all that had happened.

At first her mother was dubious.

"Oh, come on, honey. You imagined it."

"I did not. I did not."

"Baby, I know you're not crazy about Brian, but he's not an evil monster."

"Mom, you've got to believe me. When you're not around, he stares at me. And on the couch, he . . . he was touching me, Mom."

"Touching you how?"

"He put his arm around me. It was awful."

Her mother frowned. "I'll talk to him and

tell him he needs to give you your space."

Emily stared at her. "I know you love him, though I can't understand why. But you've got to believe me about this. I'm not exaggerating. Mom, I'm scared of him."

Her mother pulled her into her arms then. "All right. I don't think he means anything by it, but I'll put him on notice. Sweetie, I'm glad you told me. I want you to feel like you can come to me with anything. Anything at all."

"What if it happens again?"

Her mother frowned. "It won't."

After that, Emily was never alone in the house with Brian. Her mother made sure of that. Things seemed a bit strained for a few weeks, and a couple of times, Emily was sure her mother had been crying, but Brian never made advances toward her again. He was strict, but Emily could deal with that. She wished her mother wasn't so unhappy, but she knew Carol Gray Gillespie took her wedding vows seriously. Unless something unbearable happened, she would never leave her husband.

And so Emily planned to leave home as soon as possible. Then nothing bad could happen. Her mother and Brian could enjoy the empty nest together. As much as she loved her mother, Emily lived for the day she could escape the tension of her home. The fact that her mother encouraged her to work and attend school at a distance from home led her to the sickening conviction that her aversion to Brian was not misplaced.

And then, days before she would make her flight, Nate had asked her for a date.

"Are you okay?" Nate asked.

Emily had been silent a good five minutes. "Yeah, I'm fine."

He got up and stirred the coals, then placed an armload of wood onto the andirons. Sinking back into his chair, he eyed her cautiously. "Listen, I didn't want to bring up a lot of depressing stuff."

She lowered her eyelids and her lashes brushed her creamy cheeks. She looked defenseless, completely vulnerable.

"He didn't hurt me," she whispered.

Nate nodded. "Good. What about your mom?"

She winced, and he almost wished he hadn't asked.

"I don't know. A thousand times I wanted to ask her. She was so sure when she married him, and she kept telling me things would be great, and Brian would take care of us. But it wasn't long after the wedding that . . . she stopped laughing, Nate." Emily looked up at him with such hurt in her eyes that he tugged her toward him and pulled her into a tentative hug, over the arms of the chairs.

"I'm so sorry. I wish I could have done something."

"If I'd thought you could have, I'd have told you. But there was nothing we could do."

"Aw, Em, why didn't you write? Once you got to your job, or even that fall, when you got on campus. Why didn't you at least tell me you were okay?"

She drew a ragged breath and clung to him. "I didn't think you wanted to hear from me. You didn't make any attempt to contact me. Nate, I felt so alone and depressed. It took me my whole freshman year to sort things out with God. I came to the conclusion that Brian's interference was too much for you, and God didn't want us together."

Nate found it painful to pull air into his lungs. *How many more mistakes can I make, Lord? She needed me. Why didn't I know that?* He let his hand glide over her glossy hair, finding nothing adequate to say.

She pulled away gently and settled back in the armchair once more. "I went home for two weeks at Christmas. Mom and Brian were in Brunswick by then. It was . . . tense. I couldn't wait to leave and go back to school!" She swiped at her tears. "I thought about you all the time."

"Honest?"

She nodded, not looking at him. "I wondered if I'd ever find someone I'd feel as comfortable with."

"You were comfortable with me?" Nate's voice cracked a little, and she shot him a wary glance.

"Well, sure. Before our date, anyway. You know. We were friends for a long time."

"Yeah. I've missed that, Emily. I've missed you."

She swallowed hard and managed a shaky smile. "We're friends again now."

Nate couldn't say anything. He just sat looking into her swimming blue eyes, feeling the old, achy hope swell up inside him.

"Do you . . ." She sniffed and looked toward the fire. "Do you think we could be more than friends?"

"It's kind of hard long distance."

She nodded. "Did you . . . date much after that?"

"No. A little. I . . . pined for you for quite a while after you left. But I dated a little at the university."

"Anybody special?"

He shrugged. "The girls there seemed shallow. Oh, some of them were smart, but none of them seemed to . . . to care as much as you did."

"About you?"

"About anything. You were always passionate, Em, whether it was about homework or world peace. You're never apathetic."

She smiled. "I'll take that as a compliment."

"Anyway, I had to quit school after two years. I didn't keep touch with anyone I'd met there. The relationships didn't seem deep enough to bother."

"Date anyone here?" she asked, so low he barely heard the question.

"You know Marcy White?"

Emily jerked her chin up with a grimace. "Of course. She's from Aswontee. She was only the most popular girl in our class — always in the center of things, or throwing a hissy fit if she wasn't. How could you like her?"

Nate raised his shoulders. "She's not so bad. She grew up a little."

"How long did it last?"

"Off and on, maybe a couple of years."

"You don't still see her, do you?"

"No. She didn't . . ." He paused, wondering if it was possible Emily was jealous, and how to get out of this predicament. "She wasn't you, Em."

Emily's cheeks went pink. Her lashes swept down again, covering those big, expressive eyes. "I felt the same way. About you, I mean. Every time I started getting interested in a guy, he'd do something stupid, and I'd think, *Nate would never do that.* And that kiss . . ."

"Yes," Nate said, watching her out of the corner of his eye. "Emily, maybe it's time we put that memory to rest."

She stared at him, wide-eyed. "You mean . . ."

He smiled. "Is the idea so shocking? If I were to kiss you right now, we might both realize it was a fantasy. It wasn't really as wonderful as we thought."

"No," Emily protested. "It wasn't puppy love, and it wasn't forbidden fruit torn away. It was real."

"But we've been thinking for years that it was the most wonderful kiss on earth."

"It was. At least it was for me." Her chin came up in the stubborn gesture he'd known since they were toddlers. "Nothing could ever be as glorious as that moment."

Nate struggled with confusion. What was she saying? More important, what was she feeling? Was she talking about love in general or specific love, for a specific person, namely Nathan P. Holman, marina proprietor and erstwhile aspiring policeman?

"Em, we had a distorted picture of love. We were kids."

She closed her eyes, shaking her head. "I refuse to believe that. If you're right, then everything I've believed about true love is . . . destroyed."

Nate gulped. She was talking about true love, and she was connecting that thought to the only time he'd ever kissed her.

"All right, then." He leaned toward her and reached out to stroke her shimmering golden hair. "Let's find out."

His heart raced as he bent closer, and Emily's eyes widened for an instant. Just before his lips came within kissing range of hers, she shoved him away.

"No. I couldn't bear it if you're right. What will happen to my dreams then?"

He smiled in chagrin and surveyed her for several seconds. To all appearances, she was serious. "Fine. Let's keep the dream a little longer, then."

A hammering sounded on the porch door, and Emily jumped up, peeking out through the kitchen. She looked back over her shoulder at him. "It's the cops."

Nate rose and walked with her to the porch. Emily opened the door to Gary and another officer. "Hey, Nate, we were hoping you were still here."

"What's up, Gary?" Nate wondered if his face was red. He hoped Gary wouldn't have the opportunity to press him for details of his afternoon.

"A reporter lady climbed up the hill in high heels and sprained her ankle. Any chance you can take her and her crew over to Baxter now? She needs to get an X-ray."

"Sure." Nate glanced at Emily. "I'll see you later, Em."

"It's nearly suppertime. Better make it tomorrow."

"Well . . . if you're sure." Again the thought of the killer made him uneasy. "Mom and I will be going to prayer meeting, if you want to join us."

"I think I'll pass tonight."

Her eyes were still glinting with traces of tears. Nate hated to leave her, knowing her insides were going through at least as much turmoil as his own. Gary started down the path, and Nate could see other people on the dock, lifting the news reporter into the boat.

"I'll come out tomorrow. We'll go over that list of people connected to the party."

She nodded. "I'll be here." She let out a nervous chuckle and reached up to hug him. "Go on, you big galoot. Get out of here before I do something I'll regret."

12

The marina swarmed with tourists and fishermen ready for their first long, sunny weekend in Baxter. Nate shed his sweatshirt as he hurried about the pier, and had just rented the last canoe when his cousin Gary arrived.

"Hey, Nate," Gary called, stepping out on the dock where the runabouts and open fishing boats were moored. "Busy day?"

"Can't stand still for more than a few seconds. People are pretty excited to see the sun shining for once. What's up?"

"You went to Aswontee High School, right?"

"Yeah."

Gary fished in his pocket and pulled out a small paper bag. "Is this class ring from Aswontee?"

"Is it okay to touch it?"

"Yeah, the lab is done with it."

Nate held the ring up so he could examine

the engraving on the sides. "Definitely. From five years before I graduated."

"Take a look at the initials."

Nate squinted at the inside of the band. "RIM. Hmm. I'll bet anything that's Raven Miller, but you could check the yearbook at the library to be sure." He lowered his voice. "Where did you find that, if I'm allowed to ask?"

"In the grave on Derbin's property."

"Really?"

"We don't know how important the connection is, but I wanted to make sure it was from Aswontee before I started speculating."

"Sure. Glad I could be of help." Nate held the ring out to him. "It's in pretty good shape."

"The lab checked it for evidence. After they were done, they gave it to us so we could try to trace it. We had to clean it up a little, but of course after all this time, there wasn't any blood on it or anything." Gary pocketed the bag with the ring and grinned at Nate. "That Emily sure is something. You're a lucky guy."

Nate felt his face growing warmer than even the glaring sun would explain. He knew people were watching how he and Emily related since her return to Baxter, but he wasn't sure how obvious it was that he cared about her.

"Uh, yeah." He stooped to retie his shoelace as an excuse to avoid eye contact.

Gary's radio burbled, and he pulled it off his belt.

A petite woman with short black hair approached them from the marina. "Excuse me, the lady inside said you rent the boats. Are there any canoes left?"

Nate stood up. "No, sorry. I just rented out the last one. We've got some small motorboats, though."

"That's all right. I'm not good with motors."

"We may have a couple of kayaks left."

Gary tapped him on the shoulder. "I gotta run. There's been another burglary, at that garage out on the highway. See you later."

Nate dealt with the customer, but she decided not to rent a boat after all, so he picked up his sweatshirt and started for the store.

"There he is," his mother said as he stepped inside. She was conversing with a tall, sophisticated brunette at the counter. "Nate, you remember Pauli Derbin. She just arrived, and she's in need of a ride out to the island to meet her brother."

Pauli's thin face was accented by deep

192

blusher and a pair of dark-rimmed glasses. "Hello," she said, looking him up and down. "Would you be free to take me out to Grand Cat?"

Nate stuffed his sweatshirt on the shelf under the counter while he stalled. "Well, there've been a lot of people renting boats, so I don't know if I should leave." He sent a pleading look to his mother. "And I'm supposed to meet Emily when she's done at the library."

"I'll take her out."

Rocky stood at the end of one of the aisles of merchandise holding a two-liter bottle of soda and a large bag of chips. "I'm just heading back." He smiled broadly.

"Rocky Vigue." Nate noted the disgust in Pauli's voice as she recognized her brother's old classmate.

"Yep, that's me. You look terrific, Pauli!"

So Rocky is still infatuated by Pauline Derbin, Nate thought. His nervousness seemed to only slightly hamper his enthusiasm at seeing her again.

"I'd appreciate it if you could take her to the cottage, Rocky," said Nate. "That would be a big help."

"I suppose it will do." Pauli gathered her bags, a frown creasing her forehead.

"We can catch up on the ride out." Rocky

grinned as he laid his things on the counter. "You're running out of barbecue chips, Mrs. H."

"Oh, thank you, Rocky." She rang up his items.

Rocky and Pauli left the marina together, Pauli in the lead, Rocky fumbling with the chip bag as he tried to keep up with her long stride.

Emily was waiting for Nate outside the library. He pulled his pickup in by the walkway and got out.

"Been waiting long?"

"Not really."

"How's it going? Find anything?"

He opened the passenger side door for her.

"Nothing thrilling."

She climbed in, and Nate returned to the driver's seat and eased away from the curb.

"I looked up A Greener Maine online, just to see what they had to say for themselves. And Vital Women. There was a lot of information, but nothing pertinent as far as I could tell. So then I wrote a few e-mails and read all I could find on this area. Tourist brochures, the Web sites for the bed-and-breakfast and the hunting lodge. There's nothing sinister about this town, Nate. It's beautiful, and it's full of people three months a year. The rest of the time it's a tiny, out-of-the-way hamlet. That's all."

"Well, I have something pertinent." Nate turned onto the main road. "My cousin Gary stopped by while I was renting boats. He had a class ring they found in that grave."

"A class ring?" Emily's eyebrows shot up.

"Yeah. But it wasn't Josh's. In fact, it was a girl's. I'm pretty sure it was Raven's."

"Wow. I guess there's a good likelihood that the bones are Josh's, then."

He nodded. "The medical examiner will have to give the final word, but I'd say we can make that assumption."

They arrived at the Lumberjack just as the supper rush started and found a corner table at the back of the restaurant.

"This place looks exactly the same," said Emily. "I bet that wad of gum is still under the bench by the oak tree outside."

Nate wrinkled his nose.

A waitress approached their table and took their orders.

"That's got to be Raven's ring," Emily said. "She must have given it to Josh."

"I guess," said Nate.

"Couples did that when they went steady."

"I wouldn't know."

"Well, me neither, from personal experi-

195

ence, you understand."

"I didn't even get a ring," Nate said. "Too expensive."

She nodded, studying the menu. He wondered what would have happened if he'd had a class ring and if he'd asked Emily to wear it.

"Maybe she lost it there," said Emily.

Nate picked up the saltshaker and turned it around and around in his fingers. "Not likely." He balanced the saltshaker on top of the pepper. "You know, I don't think the police are seeing any connection between the party and Mr. Derbin's murder. But it seems to me there's something in it — you finding that grave just a few days after the old man was killed."

The waitress stepped up to their table to take their order. "What'll it be, Nate?"

"Steak?" Nate asked Emily.

Emily blinked at him. "Oh, you don't have . . ."

"It's good here. Steak," he said to the waitress.

"Well done," said Emily. "Thanks."

"Oh, no problem, honey. I'll have your order to you in just a few minutes."

When the waitress had gone again, Emily asked, "Do I know her?"

"Edna Byington. Her husband used to

teach at the elementary school."

"Oh, yeah." She pulled her notepad from her purse and pushed it across the table. "These are all the land owners, and I got the dates when they purchased their property, but we knew most of it."

Nate glanced over the list. "It was worth a try, anyway."

She flipped a page on the pad to the list of partygoers. "I'm starting to think these are the best suspects. We should cross-reference the list of people who went to the party with people who have some connection to Mr. Derbin."

"Like Raven?"

"Well, yes. She was at the party, and she took over her parents' island property. A few years later, she was the only one to convince Mr. Derbin to sell her more land."

Nate shook his head. "We don't even know for sure that the body on the hill is Josh Slate's."

"I know, but I'll be very surprised if it's not, won't you? The ring, Nate. It's gotta be."

He nodded, watching her face in the dim light. She was so beautiful, and she was *here*. Here in Baxter.

"Em . . ."

"What?"

"Do you have to leave so soon?"

She closed her notepad. "With all that's going on, I'm starting to think maybe I should take another week off."

"Can you do that?"

"Yes."

He grabbed her hand. "Do it, Em. Please?"

Her smile sent a jolt of optimism through him.

"I'll make some calls later."

When their food arrived they lapsed into silence for a while. Emily ate quietly, focusing her attention on each portion on her plate one at a time, and he remembered that from childhood, how she would work her way around the plate.

She looked up. "You're not eating."

"I ate some. I was just thinking. You still cherishing that dream, Em?"

She hesitated, looking down at her plate again. "Yeah." She breathed deeply. "I hope one day I'll find a love as powerful as the one I envisioned with you."

Nate picked up his fork and scooped up some mashed potatoes. His hope was tempered by a niggling question. How could he ever compete with this fantasy of hers if she wouldn't let him try to match it?

13

Nate let the boat putt along slowly, prolonging the ride to the island. Emily leaned back in her seat, enjoying the view of the moon rising over Baxter and reveling in the pressure of Nate's hand in hers. A perfect evening.

She sent up a silent prayer of thanks. Another memory to hold on to.

Suddenly a rogue thought flickered in her mind, and she gasped.

"What is it?" Nate leaned close and slipped his arm around her shoulders.

"I forgot to tell you. The other day — Tuesday — the day I found the bones . . ."

"Yeah?" Nate had snapped from dreamy-romantic to efficient business.

"I found a shed out back of Mr. Derbin's cottage."

"Most everybody has one."

"I know, but it was locked."

Nate shrugged. "Don't you lock yours?"

"Well, yes. Especially now. But Nate, it had a brand-new padlock on the door. At least, it looked new. It was all bright and shiny, in utter contrast to the hardware around it."

"Yeah?"

"The hinge thing on the doorjamb was solid rust, but that lock was new. I don't suppose Mr. Derbin bought a lock at your store this spring?"

"Not that I recall. So . . . you think we should tell the police?"

"I don't know. Maybe."

He raised his shoulders. "Well, that's easy. They'll be back tomorrow, I'm sure. If I see Gary or Detective Blakeney, I'll mention it."

"Thanks."

He helped her out at the dock and walked up the path with her, holding her hand. It was so like that other night, seven years ago, that Emily shivered.

"You cold?" he asked.

"No, I . . ." She glanced around at the shadowy trees.

"Brian's ghost?"

"Something like that."

At the porch he stopped and pulled her into his arms. "I'm glad you're staying, Em. I'll see you tomorrow."

"Okay."

He dropped a soft kiss on her hair, and she was glad he didn't press the issue, but when he left her and ambled down to the dock, she looked around and shuddered. Quickly she entered the porch and turned the door lock, then stood watching through the glass panes in the door as he climbed into the boat.

By arranging a second week of vacation, she'd opened the door to all sorts of possibilities. More time with Nate. Anticipation tingled in her stomach, and she inhaled deeply, watching the boat grow smaller in the shimmery path of the moon.

The wind sighed through the treetops, setting the leaves aflutter, and Emily stared into the shadows between her cottage and the Vigues'. Nothing.

She went into the kitchen and locked that door, too.

Detective Blakeney stood before the shed door on Friday morning, a fistful of keys in his hand. Nate and Emily watched as he tried several, handing the rejects to Andrew Derbin. Beside Andrew, his sister, Pauli, was biting the long, paprika-colored nail of her index finger. Gary Taylor stood back, waiting for his superior to give him an order.

"This one doesn't seem to fit." Blakeney placed another key ring in Andrew's hand. "And this one looks like a car key."

"It could be to the old boat Grandpa used to have," Andrew said.

"Well, it doesn't fit this lock." Blakeney sighed. "That's it."

Pauli's mouth sagged in disappointment. "We gathered up every key we could find in the cabin."

"And you haven't come out here since you arrived Monday?" the detective asked Andrew.

"No, sir. I didn't have a reason to. In fact, I'd forgotten all about this shed. Grandpa kept his fishing tackle in the cabin, and he's got a woodshed up nearer the dock."

"All right, Taylor."

Blakeney stepped aside, and Gary raised the crowbar he'd brought with him.

"Sorry, Andrew. If there's nothing suspicious inside, I'll fix this for you."

Pauli smiled up at Gary. "Well, aren't you nice! But don't worry about that. There's no reason on earth for Grandpa to have put a new lock on this old shed. And if there were, he'd have had the key lying around in plain sight."

Gary went to work, and they all waited in silence. Nate caught Emily's eye, and she shrugged. He wondered if she felt guilty for causing this destruction.

Gary worked the blade under the old hasp and pried it from the wood with a tearing sound that sent shivers down Nate's spine.

"All right, everyone stand back." Blakeney took a flashlight from his belt, switched it on, and reached for the door handle.

He swung the door open, and Nate made himself stay put, not leaning in behind Gary to see, but his cousin let out a low whistle.

"What is it?" Andrew asked.

Pauli pushed up beside Gary and took his arm. "Let me see."

He edged sideways so she could look, and Pauli was reduced to silence.

Nate glanced at Emily, and they both turned back to the opening.

"Why on earth . . ." Andrew shook his head and looked at the detective in disbelief.

"Take a look," Blakeney said to Nate.

He and Emily stepped forward and peered inside. The shed was crammed with tools, chainsaws, and a gas generator.

"Grandpa didn't put this stuff here." Pauline raised her chin, ready to defend her grandfather against anyone who said otherwise.

Gary scratched his head and glanced at

Blakeney. "You thinking what I'm thinking?"

"That theft over at Northern Trails Paper a couple of weeks ago?"

"Yeah. And don't forget," Gary said, "we're pretty sure that was the same thief as the break-in at Hagerton Lumber in Aswontee."

Pauline turned on her brother with an icy stare. "What do you know about this, Andrew?"

"Nothing."

"Oh, sure. You've been here four days, and you're absolutely ignorant. Why don't you ever tell the truth?"

Andrew's face went scarlet. "I am telling the truth. I had no idea this stuff was here."

Pauli turned on her heel and stalked toward the cottage.

Andrew pulled in a deep breath. "I'm sorry, Detective Blakeney. If I knew anything about this, I'd tell you."

Emily spent two hours that afternoon cleaning the upstairs bedrooms of the cottage, then changed into her swimsuit. As she headed down to the dock armed with sunscreen, a towel, a water bottle, and a fat novel, she saw a familiar boat tying up.

"Felicia! Join me for a swim?"

"No, thanks, Emily. I'm too busy. I'm publishing an extra tomorrow. I have two hours, not a minute more, to get my final proofs done."

"Then you'd better hop to it."

"I was hoping to get a quick statement from you."

"What about?"

Felicia laughed. "The shed, of course. Oh, and I interviewed Pauli and Andrew Derbin yesterday. They told me they haven't decided yet if they want to sell their interest in the island. To tell you the truth, I got the impression they've been fighting about it."

"What does that have to do with me?" Emily asked.

"I went over there just now to get a little clarification, and the cops were there again. That Blakeney seems to think you're some kind of a crime magnet."

"What?" Emily stared at her. "That's crazy."

"Maybe not. Blakeney says this island's had more crime since you came back last weekend than it's had in its entire previous history."

Emily shook her head and sat down in a lawn chair. "I'm sure he's joking. And I can't help it."

"Can't help what? Uncovering crimes? Is

that what you do in Hartford?"

"No, in Hartford I'm just a reporter. I get an assignment, and I go write about it. But here . . . well, can I help it if someone's been committing crimes on Grand Cat and no one else has caught on yet?"

"Are you saying the other folks here turn a blind eye to crime?"

"No, I'm not saying that at all."

"Well, Blakeney says you've got the mind of either a master criminal or a top-notch detective, he's not sure which yet."

"He was joking, right? He can't think I set up any of this!"

Felicia leaned toward her eagerly. "What if he does?"

"Oh, come on, that's stupid! And don't quote me. I'm not about to start a printer's ink feud with Blakeney. I'm sure he's a capable officer and will get to the bottom of this."

"Meaning the stolen stuff in Henry Derbin's shed? Or Henry's murder? Or that skeleton you found up on the hill?"

"All of it."

Felicia shook her head. "You've got to admit, that's a lot of intrigue for a sleepy place like Baxter.

Emily gritted her teeth and sought for a topic that would divert Felicia. "So, Andrew and Pauline aren't selling?"

"I guess not. Pauli said the Greens approached them again. She didn't say how much they offered, but she said it was tempting. And I'm quoting that in the *Journal*."

"But they didn't accept?"

"No. Pauli said they're going to wait awhile, let the dust settle, and get Mr. Derbin's estate all tied up, then they might think about it. But the Greens don't want to wait."

"There's nothing they can do about it if the Derbins don't want to sell." Emily smoothed waterproof sunblock over her arms and shoulders.

"The Greens held a press conference in Bangor yesterday."

"Oh? Did you go?"

"No, but I spoke to Barton Waverly by telephone afterward. He says A Greener Maine is going to sponsor several events this summer to raise money. They want to buy this island and some shore land, too, and turn it into that wilderness preserve they've been talking about."

Emily sighed. "The property owners won't like that. None of them will sell willingly."

"I'm not so sure, if the price is high enough. And the Greens might get a large tract from one of the paper companies."

"I wonder how that would affect property values."

"That's just what I'm hearing everywhere I go. That and, will it stop them from using their land any way they want to?"

"You mean, could someone develop his property later or sell it for another purpose?" Emily asked.

"That's right. Everyone wants to know if A Greener Maine would oppose them if they disagreed on land use."

"There are no easy answers to questions like that," Emily said. "The Greens ought to look for another parcel of land. Far away from Baxter."

"I think they are looking at a few other locations for the wilderness preserve, but this is their top choice." Felicia ran a hand through her short, brown hair, then smiled. "I wish I had a reporter experienced with issues like that. I confess, I've had to do a lot of research already on this, and I'm still confused about land-use regulations. I don't suppose you'd consider writing an article or two about all the goings-on out here?"

Emily quickly quashed the flicker of interest that tempted her. "I'm on vacation. Besides, zoning and land use aren't my turf."

"Guest column?"

"Not a chance." Emily stowed the sunscreen under her chair and stood. "Right now I'm going to jump in the lake."

Felicia smiled and reached for the painter that held her boat to the dock. "I'd better get moving or that extra won't come out."

That evening Emily donned her sneakers and jeans and wended her way slowly up the hillside. The trail was distinct, now that dozens of people had flattened the grass and broken off branches that protruded into the path.

Why she was drawn back to the hilltop grave, she couldn't have said exactly. She'd brought along her cell phone, and could have used the excuse that she missed Nate, who was still busy at the marina, and wanted to talk to him. But no one badgered her for an explanation, and she didn't try to unravel the interwoven inklings and questions that compelled her to revisit the site.

She climbed above the trees into the open area at the summit and stopped. A woman was sitting on the ground inside the lopsided circle of yellow crime scene tape. The tape was broken in several places now and fluttered in the breeze.

Emily hesitated, then approached, making

no effort to silence her steps. Raven had positioned herself a couple of yards from the excavation. Her long, dark hair rippled as the wind chased across the hilltop, and she stirred, turning toward Emily.

"Hello."

"Hi." Emily stopped beside one of the stakes holding the tape. "Would you rather I left?"

"That depends."

Raven stood and brushed off the seat of her denim cutoffs. She walked over to stand beside Emily and turned to face the hole in the earth.

"Why did you come up here?" Raven asked.

Emily swallowed and shook her head slightly. She could say, *God brought me here,* but that would sound odd to Raven, she was sure. "I'm still trying to put it together in my mind. It's . . . surreal."

"You must see a lot of strange things in your line of work."

"Not like this. I've covered some crime stories, but . . ."

The rays of the setting sun glinted on wet streaks that marred Raven's smooth cheeks.

"Are you all right?" Emily asked.

Raven frowned, staring once more toward the excavation site, then shook her head.

"No. Today was . . . too much."

"Worse than yesterday?"

"Yesterday was pretty hard." Raven raised her hand and smeared fresh tears from her cheek. "Then there's Andrew."

"Andrew?"

She let out a mirthless chuckle. "He about bit my head off today."

"Whatever for?"

"He told me last fall that he'd talk to his grandfather about selling me more land for the retreat center. Now that Mr. Derbin's dead, I figured Andrew would be willing to sell to me. But today he said he and Pauli haven't decided yet whether they want to sell or not."

"And that's a huge disappointment?"

Raven sighed. "It's not just that. It's . . . all the things that have happened this week."

"Is it . . . Josh?"

"I feel so guilty!" Raven whipped around to face Emily, the furrows at the corners of her eyes giving her the air of a much older woman. "We fought that night, you know. And he . . . disappeared. Afterward, I wanted to die. I kept wondering if it was my fault. If I hadn't fought with Josh, he'd have stayed with the others, and he would have gotten home all right."

"It's not your fault."

"How do you know that? Don't you believe in fate or . . . or karma or something?"

"I believe in God."

Raven sighed. "For the past few years, I've put my soul into the retreat center. I thought if I could help other women slay their demons, then it would help me, and I'd have peace, too."

"But it hasn't worked that way?"

Raven shook her head. The breeze blew her hair into her face, and she impatiently shoved it back, turning slightly so it would flow behind her. "This has brought back so many memories. Bitterness. Grief. And then I made the mistake of trying to deal with Andrew today. I figured he wouldn't stay here long, and I'd better take advantage of his being here, before someone like that Greener Maine group strikes a deal with him and Pauli."

Emily wished she had her reporter's notebook, but she said nothing, schooling her mind to file away Raven's words for future pondering.

Raven scowled. "I reminded Andrew today that he made me a promise, and he reneged. Then that snooty Pauli got into it. She dressed me down in front of one of my staff, saying it's not up to Andrew alone what will be done with the property. He was embarrassed, but I think that was her intention."

"Sometimes you just have to wait," Emily said softly.

"What do you mean?"

"I saw Andrew today, too. He and Pauli are dealing with a lot right now. Their grandfather's death and settling the estate, the discovery of a body and a hoard of stolen goods on their property . . ."

"I heard about that."

"Give them a while to catch their breath."

Raven sighed and pulled out a resigned smile.

"I suppose when things get you down, you pray."

Her comment caught Emily off guard. "I do."

"Does it help you?"

"Yes."

Raven began to walk toward the path, and Emily kept pace with her. As they approached the tree line, Raven stopped and faced her again.

"You know, since high school, I've studied every religion there is, and I concluded that being at one with nature is the only honest way for human beings to be at peace."

Emily sent up a quick, silent prayer. "Pardon my saying so, Raven, but you don't seem to be at peace tonight."

"You're right. I've dabbled in alternative spirituality for years now, but nothing rings true. Even my ultimate solution . . . unity with nature . . . leaves me feeling . . ." Suddenly she looked into Emily's eyes with a piercing gaze. "Do you think a person can truly become part of nature?"

"You mean . . . without dying?" Emily felt the conversation was going off into a tangential world.

Raven rotated and stared behind them, back up the hill. "Maybe that's it. If that was Josh's body lying there, I guess he was united with nature. He's at peace now."

"Do you really believe that?" Emily asked.

There was a long silence, and then Raven whispered, "I'd like to, but . . . No."

Emily touched her shoulder lightly. "Why don't you come down to my place and have a cup of cocoa with me? I'd like to show you what God says about peace. Peace that's greater than our understanding."

14

Emily walked from the marina to the *Journal* office. As she neared the little shingled building, she saw Felicia park in front of it and hurry to the door. Emily picked up her pace and arrived just as Felicia turned the key.

"Mind if I come in and use your morgue?"

"Sure. You're welcome anytime." Felicia swung the door open and plopped her briefcase and a tote bag on her desk.

"Where've you been?" Emily asked. The file cabinets that comprised the newspaper's back files were still in the same corner, though they seemed to have nearly doubled in number since Carol Gray had sold the *Journal* to Felicia.

"The state police spokesman held a press conference this morning."

"You went all the way to Augusta?"

"Yes, I wanted to get it firsthand and be sure I had a chance to ask a few questions."

"So, what did he say?"

Felicia sighed. "They've identified the body you found. The second one, I mean."

"Who is it?" Emily asked.

"How bad do you want to know?"

Emily smiled. "Badly."

"I thought so."

"No, I mean, you should use the adverbial form. *How badly.*"

"I knew that."

"Come on, Felicia. Don't make me stay over here to watch it on the evening news with Nate and Connie tonight." Emily pulled a folder from the drawer. "I guess I could call the city desk at the *Bangor Daily* and ask them —"

Felicia clapped her hand to her heart. "You're cruel."

"So, tell me."

"Will you write a follow-up story for my next edition about the stolen goods in Henry Derbin's shed?"

"No."

Felicia stamped her foot and sat down in her swivel chair. "I'm really stressed, Emily. I know you're on vacation, but I can't think of a single person in town who could give me the help I need this week . . ."

"How about Diane Quinn? She's still

teaching at the elementary school, isn't she?"

"Yes."

"Well, school's out. She must have the summer off. She's intelligent and up to speed in composition."

"She and her husband went to visit their daughter in Tennessee."

"Oh."

"I don't suppose your mother would come up and help me for a —"

"Mom is in the throes of a business start-up. She's planning to open a bookstore in Brunswick."

Felicia drooped in her chair and rested her chin on her hand. "It's Joshua Slate."

"Thought so."

"The timing is horrible. One day too late to make it into my extra!"

"I saw the extra." Emily opened a drawer on one of the cabinets. "It looked great."

"Thanks, but every paper in Maine will run this new story before I do. It's so frustrating! I'm thinking of going to press twice a week."

"Every week?" Emily stared at her. "That would be a lot more work."

"I know." Felicia sighed. "Charlie Benton could handle the advertising, I think, but I really, *really* need another reporter. Or at least a stringer. Here I've got this hot story on the island corpse, and the fire department auxiliary is having a big planning meeting for the field day tonight. Then Monday, the school board is meeting — there's so much going on with regular business in town! My coverage of that has suffered since this crime wave on Grand Cat started, I'll tell you."

Emily sat on the edge of the desk Charlie Benton used to lay out the ads each week. Things were playing out the way she'd feared, and the news would be a shock to the Slate family and others who had known Joshua, while at the same time bringing relief from the years of questioning. She wanted Felicia to have time to write the articles with care and sensitivity.

"Tell you what. I'll cover the auxiliary's planning meeting tonight, and I might even be persuaded to report on the school board meeting Monday, but I don't want to cover the theft story. It will be time consuming, and . . . well, I'm already closer to it than I want to be."

Felicia's eyes sparkled as she ruffled through her notebook and scribbled on a sticky pad. "Thank you! You're saving my life. And if it's any consolation, Blakeney *was* kidding about you being a criminal mastermind. He thinks you're brilliant. Here's the contact information for those two meetings. Working with you is going to be great, Emily!"

"Well, try to find someone else you can train in a hurry. I'm not staying long."

"I will. But you're bailing me out in a big way."

"This crime frenzy should calm down eventually." Emily opened the folder she held and flipped through the clippings. "You may not have enough news for two issues a week after all of this is over."

"I think I will. If I could get another reporter, I'd extend my coverage to Aswontee and a few of the other small towns. No one gets enough coverage in the *BDN* up here. And that would open up a whole new base of advertisers for us."

"Sounds like you've given this a lot of thought."

"I have."

Emily stood up. "Well, since you're the one writing the story about Josh Slate's remains being identified, you'll probably need this folder for background. I'd like to run a few photocopies, though, if you don't mind."

Felicia glanced at the label. "Is that what you came to look at?"

"Yes. Just refreshing my memory on some of the details."

Nate walked out the back door with a gigantic mound of life jackets in his arms. He detoured around Andrew Derbin's long legs as he made his way to the party boat pier. A customer wanted the boat ready to go in half an hour, and he had to check the gas and all the safety features.

Andrew sat on one bench, and his sister sat on another, ten feet away, on the other side of the marina's back door. Both were engrossed in their copies of the extra edition of the *Journal.* They'd ridden over from the island with him and Emily after Nate delivered the morning's mail, and the first thing they'd done was buy the *Journal.* At first Nate had found it odd that they'd bought identical papers, but now it made sense.

"Why did you have to say that to her?" Pauli jabbed her finger at a story below the fold on page one.

"Dry up." Andrew turned to the back page to continue reading the article.

"Oh, that's brilliant. You have the vocabulary of a Neanderthal. I don't understand how you ever got that cushy job at the statehouse."

"One of many things you don't understand," Andrew snarled.

Nate stepped down to the deck of the party pontoon boat and stowed the life jackets. The locker already held half a dozen. *So we need four more,* he noted. The boat's capacity was twenty people, and the marina was required to supply a flotation device for every customer on the rented vessel.

He headed back toward the store.

"Are you going back out to Grand Cat?" Andrew asked as he drew near.

"I can if you need me to."

"Not yet!" Pauli jumped to her feet. "We need groceries, Andrew."

"Oh, yeah, yeah. Nate, have you got a small motorboat we can rent for the next couple of days?"

"Sure."

"I wish Grandpa had kept his boat." Pauli folded her newspaper. "I'm done with this, Nate. Do you want to sell it again?"

"Uh . . ."

"You idiot." Andrew snatched the paper from his sister's hand.

"What, you need two?"

"No, but you don't resell newspapers."

"Wanna bet?" Pauli shaded her eyes and

squinted toward the island. "Is that Rocky Vigue?"

"Looks like it," Nate said.

"Watch this."

Pauli walked out on the longest pier and stood waving while Rocky brought his speedboat in. Sure enough, Pauli drew him in like a magnet.

"Hi, Pauli," he said as soon as he'd cut the motor. He tossed her the painter, and she tied it up for him while Rocky clambered onto the dock.

"Want to buy a paper?" She held out her creased *Journal*.

"Nah, I already read Dad's. That's a good picture of you and Andrew. How come you're not selling the land now?"

Pauli glared at him. "Because we don't want to."

"Says you," Andrew shouted.

"So, you want to," Rocky said, looking toward Andrew, then switching his gaze back to Pauli, "but you don't?"

"I didn't say that." She strolled toward the marina, and Rocky followed her.

"Did you read the story about the Greens?" he panted as they reached the back deck. "Sounds like they'd give you a pile of dough for that property."

"Oh, yeah, they're raising all kinds of

money for their project," Andrew said.

"We're not sure selling to them would be in our best interest." Pauli splayed her hands and examined her fingernails.

"Yeah, maybe we'll sell to someone else," Andrew said, eyeing Pauli warily.

She threw him a warning look. "If you think I'm going to let Raven Miller have that land for a song —"

"Oh, and I suppose you'd let it go to Rand Pooler, so he can expand the boys' camp."

"Is that so outrageous?"

"Yes. People don't want boy campers overrunning their private space, do they, Rocky?"

Rocky gulped. "Well . . . my folks wouldn't like it, I guess. Too noisy."

"Right!"

Nate stood back as Pauli marched past him toward the store, tossing her *Journal* into the barrel that served as a trash can.

"Hey, wait," Rocky cried. "I came to get a new strap for that life belt. You guys want to go waterskiing this afternoon?"

"Sounds good." Andrew stood up and stretched.

Rocky followed Pauli into the store. "Wait. Pauli, wait. Did you hear what I said?"

Nate and Andrew looked at each other. Andrew was the first to crack a smile.

"I don't know why he likes her."

"Think she'll go waterskiing?"

"Probably. She never would give Rocky the time of day, but she does like to ski. And he's got a great boat this year."

"It's his father's."

"Oh, right. Pardon me. Marvin's got a great boat at their cottage this summer. And we have none." Andrew winked at Nate. "My sister may find Rocky despicable, but she's not above letting him show her a good time."

"Rocky's not so bad."

"No, but Pauli's stuck up." Andrew folded his *Journal* and tucked it under his arm. "Rocky and I used to be best friends, all through school. But here's the difference between him and me: I left Baxter and made something of myself. Rocky stayed here and vegetated."

Andrew opened the door and went inside.

Like me, Nate thought. *If I'd left here and found some way to finish school, would Emily look at me differently now?*

The party boat customers would be arriving soon. Maybe after he saw them off on their outing, he could spend some time with Emily. He wondered if she had been waterskiing since she moved away. Or maybe she'd like to go snorkeling. There was a quiet cove at the bottom of a rocky ledge a mile or so down the lake. Maybe they could run down there and swim and have a picnic supper.

Nate went into the marina. His mother was talking to a knot of customers in the aisle. Early arrivals for the party boat? Nate glanced around the store and saw a few more customers browsing. Pauli was loading a shopping basket in the food section, with Rocky carrying the basket for her. Andrew was examining the fishing tackle display.

The front door opened, and Gary and another trooper came inside. Gary pulled his hat off and stood blinking for a moment, then stepped toward him, and Nate went to meet them.

"Hey, Nate, we'll need a boat," Gary said.

"What's up?"

"Well . . ." Gary shot a quick glance around the store then froze. "That's Rocky Vigue, isn't it?"

"Yeah."

Gary nodded and turned to speak quietly to the other trooper. Then he looked back at Nate. "Scratch that boat, Nate. Thanks. We'll make this quick."

Nate swallowed hard and watched them walk toward the food section. Pauli was

225

laughing as she piled containers of yogurt into the nearly overflowing basket. Her mouth went slack when she caught sight of Gary, and she stopped laughing.

There was a momentary lull in the conversation among Connie's group, and Gary's distinct words could be heard throughout the store.

"Richard Vigue, you are under arrest. You have the right to remain silent. If you give up the right to remain silent, anything you say can and will be used against you in a court of law. You have the right to an attorney. If you desire an attorney and cannot —"

"I do!" Rocky's face was pale. "I want one."

Gary nodded. "All right. Turn around, Rocky, and put your hands on the refrigerator door."

Pauli found her voice at last. "This is ridiculous. You're arresting him? For what?"

"We'll start with theft and criminal trespass," Gary said.

"Not murder?"

"No, Ms. Derbin. Today we're dealing with the theft of the equipment found in your grandfather's shed."

Andrew walked over and stood beside Rocky. "Where are you taking him?"

"To the police station in Aswontee, for now."

"Tell my dad!" Rocky's face was distorted with anguish as he looked over his shoulder at Andrew.

"I will." Andrew stepped toward his old friend, but the second police officer moved between them.

"Stand back, please."

"Tell my dad to come to Aswontee," Rocky called.

"I'll tell him."

Gary and the other officer took Rocky in handcuffs out to their patrol car. Nate inhaled deeply and looked toward his mother. Her face was pale, but she managed a strained smile to the customers near her.

"Well, now, about the refreshments on the boat . . ."

"Come on," Andrew said to his sister. "We need to find Marvin."

"I'm not ready."

"Let Nate bring you out later, then. I'm taking Rocky's boat out and telling Marvin what happened."

"Hey," Pauli called after him, "do you suppose Marvin will let us use the boat to go waterskiing while he's bailing Rocky out?"

15

The air was pleasantly warm and the sky clear when Nate and Emily arrived at her dock after church the next evening. They sat in lawn chairs on the screened-in porch, where they could watch the last golden rays of sun slant down on the lake from behind the island. Nate saw most of his sunsets from the marina's back deck, and the water took on new tints and shadows from this perspective.

Emily brought out a pitcher of lemonade and two paper cups.

"Nate, I was thinking, what if Mr. Derbin found that grave?"

"What if?"

"It would make sense. If he found Josh Slate's body, and someone else knew he was going to report it to the police . . ." She filled the cups and handed one to him before sitting down.

Nate took the cup, sipping slowly while he

thought. "That would definitely tie every-thing together. Unless he knew about it for some time but wasn't planning on reporting it. Forbidding people to go on his property, and all."

"But he's always been that way, since way before Josh disappeared." She fished an elastic out of her pocket and pulled her hair back into a ponytail.

"You're right. Even when I was a kid, no one was allowed up the hill or in the swamp. Dad figured it was because he didn't want the herons disturbed." Nate drained his cup and set it on the floor beside his chair. "I really don't think Mr. Derbin could have had anything to do with Josh's death, though."

"But what about Andrew and Pauli? They keep going back and forth on whether or not the land is for sale."

He'd been thinking about their argument at the marina. "Do you think they're chang-ing their minds because the secret's out about Josh? Before they didn't dare sell, but maybe now it doesn't matter."

"I don't know. But Andrew and Pauli were both away when Mr. Derbin was killed," said Emily. "Pauli hasn't been back for years, and you said Andrew hadn't been down yet this summer."

"Well, not that I know of. And when he does come, Andrew usually comes straight to me for a ride out to the cottage."

"How about Raven, then?"

Nate gritted his teeth and watched the sky darken. The first star popped out, then another, and a loon sent its plaintive call echoing down the lake. "She was the last person known to see Josh alive. I hate to think of her as a suspect, but the police probably are. And if she knew the body was there, that would give her added reason to want that land. To make certain the grave was never found."

Emily held her cup steady on her knee. "She did seem quite shaken by the discovery. Hey, if she and Josh were breaking up, do you think there was someone else involved?"

"A love triangle? Jealousy is a strong motive." Nate slid his feet forward, stretching his legs out.

"If we'd been in their class, we'd know all this," said Emily. "High school girls usually do a lot of talking about who's going out with whom."

"Speaking of which, how about Rocky? He used the Derbin land to hide the things he stole until he could sell them. Maybe he had more than that to hide."

Emily shook her head, a frown wrinkling the smooth skin between her eyebrows. "I'll admit, I was pretty surprised by that."

"Me, too," said Nate. "He's not exactly shifty-eyed. It's too bad he got into this. He's a nice guy."

"Or is he?"

Nate pondered for a moment. He'd thought he knew Rocky, but the man was obviously good at keeping secrets.

"I think those are our most likely suspects," said Emily. "Andrew, Raven, and Rocky. And I guess Pauli, but she hasn't been around. And frankly, she doesn't seem like the type."

"None of them do. That's the thing. I kind of dislike pinning the title *murderer* on anyone I've known most of my life."

"I know."

Nate eased out of his chair and walked to the edge of the porch. "Wow, look at the stars, Em."

Thousands of white pinpoints dotted the black sky.

She came to stand beside him. "I've missed this. Things as simple and beautiful as this. I'd love to live out here in the country again."

"Yeah?" Nate's voice caught, and he slipped his arm around her shoulders.

"I think about it sometimes. But I can't see how I could support myself away from the city."

He turned around and sat on the ledge below the screen windows, so they were at eye level. "I wish you could come back to stay."

She smiled. "It's been great coming back to Baxter and being on the island again, but I admit the chaos has taken away some of the joy."

He reached up and stroked back a wisp of hair she'd missed when she corralled the ponytail. "I'm sorry. But even with all that's happened, I can't help being glad you're here."

"Oh, Nate, that's sweet. I've thought a lot about you, too. Us. Together again. But . . . don't you think that if we tried to pick up where we left off seven years ago, the same thing would happen?"

He swallowed hard, not sure he wanted to follow her line of reasoning. Better to seize the moment, with Emily, the stars, and the still, warm night. But with Emily, romance always held a tragic note, and he knew that if they couldn't dispel it, their relationship would never move past where they were at the moment . . . wistful, but destined for loneliness.

A jab of rebellion struck his heart so hard it hurt. He captured her hand and stared at her, forcing her to look into his eyes.

"What do you mean 'would happen'?"

"You know."

"No, I'm dense. Spell it out for me."

She squirmed a little, but he held her hand firmly and kept her close. No more avoiding the subject. It was time.

"Wouldn't the complications of adulthood spoil it?" He leaned closer to catch every word. "It wouldn't be how I always imagined it. That's what you tried to tell me before, and I think you were right about that."

Nate leaned back and focused on her evasive eyes. Was she closing the door on that dream forever? Was this her way of saying it was time for him to forget about it?

Maybe coming here and seeing him again had settled the matter for her, and he was no longer her ideal. When she went back to Hartford, maybe she'd feel ready to take up with someone else, since she was no longer cherishing the memory of what they'd had.

The sudden, bleak emptiness shocked him. How could she abandon the dream? Ever since she'd told him she'd held out for the love they'd almost had, it had haunted his thoughts and become part of the unrealized longing he'd felt all these years. Now she was giving that up.

"Em, you can't just throw it away like that."

"I'm not tossing anything. I'm just being realistic. A girl's idea of love is distorted at best. And at worst . . ."

Nate stood up, and she jumped back, staring at him.

"What did I say?"

He plowed a hand through his hair and groped for the right words. "You're right that love isn't all thrills and poetry. But when you think of love, don't think of all the disappointing relationships you've seen. Think of . . . think of your mom and dad. They had the real thing."

She pressed her lips together and turned to stare out at the water.

"Yeah," she whispered. "Yeah, they did."

"Mine, too. Emily, I don't want to let you leave here again unless we find out for sure."

"About love?"

"About us. Why couldn't we find the same kind of love our folks had? If God wants it to happen, it could. It really could."

She swung toward him and stared, her lips parted and the stars reflected in her pupils.

"But what if . . ."

"What?"

"What if it's not meant to be?"

"Then we'll know." He stepped toward her, reaching for her. "One kiss, Em. That's all I'm asking. Let go of the memory and trade it for reality. If it's awful, then, fine . . . we'll stay friends, okay?"

He thought a smile quivered at the corners of her mouth, but it was quite dark now.

"What if it's not?"

"Not awful?"

"Yes."

He willed his heart to slow down. "Well, if it's . . . magical . . ."

She laughed, a sweet laugh of approval, and he felt hope flutter inside him, then surge with more confidence than he'd known since Emily went away.

He ran his fingertips over the smoothness of her cheek and slid them toward her ear, where her satiny hair gleamed. She gulped and brought her hands up to rest lightly on each side of his collar, and he bent his head. Her eyes widened for an instant, then she closed them, and as his lips touched hers, he felt her hands slip up behind his neck and hold him, close and trusting. She returned his caress with tenderness that melted any reservations lingering in Nate's subconscious. This was right.

He pulled away and sighed, waiting for

her reaction.

She opened her eyes and stood still for a moment, looking up at him, then opened her mouth. "You were so wrong."

"I was?"

"Totally."

"How?"

"That was . . ." She looked away and inhaled, then tipped her head back and met his gaze. "It was . . . everything I remembered and imagined. If you can't see that, Nathan, Pierce Holman, you're crazy."

"I'm not crazy. I love you, Em."

He pulled her back into his arms and kissed her again.

16

Nate pounded on Emily's cottage door shortly before noon on Monday.

"Hey! What's up?"

"Felicia wanted me to deliver this when I made my rounds." He held out a folded sheet of paper, and Emily took it, a bit shy at standing so close to him again after last's night's discovery. Nate's crooked smile made her stomach lurch, and she turned her attention to the note.

"She wants me to go back with you and help her this afternoon."

"That doesn't surprise me. She's swamped."

Emily frowned. "I'm doing the school board meeting for her tonight."

"Yeah, but the paper comes out tomorrow, and she has to remake the front page."

"Why?"

"Big news. Rocky's confessed to stealing all those things in the shed."

"All of it?"

"Yup. They found his fingerprints all over it, so I guess he didn't see a point in holding out any longer. He was arraigned this morning, and his lawyer gave Felicia a detailed phone interview."

"Wow, she must be excited."

"She is. This is one story the big papers aren't paying much attention to, so she's got an exclusive. But Rocky admits to stealing stuff from one of the paper company storage buildings and several cottages."

"Not here on Blue Heron?"

"No, over Moosehead way. I don't know about the break-in at the garage in Aswontee. Maybe he did that, too."

"Well, I suppose I can help her this afternoon. At least she's got an air conditioner in the office."

"Yeah, it's hot out. It's not bad on the water, though."

"Let me grab a sandwich, okay?"

"Why don't you just eat with Mom and me?" Nate asked. "I'm almost at the end of my run. Two stops, and we'll head back to the marina and grab a bite. Then you can go help Felicia, and I'll start loading the parts of your new dock."

"It's here?"

"The truck was unloading when I left an

hour ago. I figured I'd do my mail run and spend the afternoon putting the dock in. I'll use the pontoon boat to carry all the parts out here."

Emily climbed into the cabin cruiser and put on her life jacket. "That's a big job. Can you do it alone?"

Nate winced and looked toward the Vigues' cottage. "I was going to ask Rocky to help me. But I think I can hire the Kimmel boys, and maybe their dad, too. If that's not enough muscle, there are a couple of high school boys I might be able to get."

"Taking down the old dock will probably be the worst of it."

"Yeah, well, say good-bye to it." Nate grinned and shoved off. "This is probably the last time you'll ever see it."

Emily sat in silence while they puttered to Andrew and Pauli's dock. Andrew came out to meet them, and Nate handed him two envelopes and an Augusta newspaper.

"It's your grandfather's mail. Sorry."

"That's okay. Hey, any news about Rocky?" Andrew asked.

"Yeah, he's confessed."

Andrew leaned on the dock piling and scowled. "Stupid idiot. Never thought of him as a thief."

Nate nodded. "It wasn't brilliant. He said

he knew your grandfather never went out back anymore, and he figured no one would know. I guess he stole all that stuff this spring, and was planning to fence it soon, but with cops all over the island this past week, he decided he'd better wait."

Andrew sighed. "He's smarter than that. He may not look it, but he is."

"I never thought he was stupid."

"Man!" Andrew slammed his fist down on top of the piling. "I told him last summer to come down to Augusta, and I could get him a job. You know what he said?"

Nate shook his head.

"He said he didn't want to work as hard as I do."

"That's too bad."

"You got that right. Rocky used to be a sharp kid, but he got lazy. His parents didn't help. They always made things too easy for him." Andrew turned away, his mouth set in a hard line.

The last stop was at Camp Dirigo, and Emily sat in the boat while Nate carried two bins of mail to the camp office. He'd said nothing so far about last night. But then, were any words necessary?

He came back and hopped down to the deck, winking at her as he started the motor. They edged away from the wharf, and he reached for her hand. Emily smiled up at him, and a flash of knowledge flew between them. She sat back wondering if she had ever felt so utterly content.

They ate a light lunch in the Holmans' kitchen, and Emily lingered over her tea while Nate went next door to relieve his mother at the marina. Connie bustled in through the back door a minute later.

"Emily, what fun! I hope Nate gave you a decent meal."

"It was great. Salad and tuna sandwiches. I made one for you."

"Thanks so much." Connie pulled the salad bowl toward her. "We've been so busy lately, Nate and I have discussed taking Allison on full time for the summer. Nate has to be out on the lake so much, it wears me out to try to tend the store and post office and deal with the rentals." She served herself salad as she talked, then looked at Emily. "Something's different."

"What?" Emily asked.

"You. You look . . . sparkly."

Emily laughed.

"No, I mean it. You're always so pensive, but today . . ."

"I'm just happy."

"Does my son have anything to do with that?"

241

Emily hesitated and felt her cheeks warm. "He has pretty much everything to do with that."

Connie leaned toward her with a joyful grin. "Let me hug you, you dear girl! You've no idea how glad that makes me."

Emily sat at Felicia's computer two hours later, typing community news briefs. Charlie Benton, Felicia's advertising manager, sat across the room, contacting potential advertisers by phone and attempting to convince them that they couldn't afford not to buy ads in the *Journal.* He leaned back so that his shoulder-length, graying hair hung down behind his chair back, and he studied the ceiling as he talked, occasionally waving a pencil around and punctuating his sentences with stabs of the pencil.

The door to the little office swung open, and Raven Miller entered with a burst of hot air. Her long hair was pinned off her neck in a cool updo, and Emily couldn't help noticing that her bare legs were evenly tanned. Apparently Charlie couldn't help noticing, either. He sat up straighter and put more enthusiasm into his voice as he clinched a sale and began to scribble the specifications for Aswontee Outfitters' new ad.

"Where's Felicia?" Raven asked, looking from Emily to Charlie and back, then settling on Emily and pulling up a chair.

"Gone to the island. The police are removing Rocky's loot from Mr. Derbin's shed."

"Isn't that wild?" Raven leaned forward. "I was absolutely floored when I heard. Rocky Vigue! Imagine."

Emily nodded. "Shows you really never know a person, doesn't it?"

"I'll say. The first thing I did was take inventory."

Emily couldn't help smiling. "Anything missing?"

"No. I guess he only ripped off people he didn't know."

"Can I help you with something?"

"Maybe." Raven opened the jute bag slung over her shoulder and pulled out an envelope. "I've got the press kit here for the speaker we're hosting the third week in July."

"All right. I'll see that Felicia gets it."

"Thanks. It's kind of a big deal."

"How big?" Emily asked.

"So big it's the highest speaker fee I've ever paid. Ever hear of maharishi Yagnev?"

"Don't think so."

"Oh, he's very big in the spiritualist world."

Emily inclined her head slightly. "You have a man coming to instruct your campers?"

"Yes, and we still have some slots open for the retreat. Felicia said she's going to distribute the paper in a larger area from now on, so, since circulation is going up, I thought maybe we'd attract a few local women. If not, the ads will at least give us some PR in the community."

Emily took the envelope with misgivings and laid it on Felicia's stack of unopened mail. "I'll tell her. She should be back soon."

"Thanks." Raven slumped back in the chair. "Are you going to be here all day?"

"No, I just came over to answer the phone and do some typing for Felicia. She's been so busy, she couldn't handle it all today. I'm covering the school board this evening, too. But as soon as Felicia comes back, I thought I'd run back out to the island, take a swim, eat supper, and change before the meeting."

"Well, I could take you to your cottage."

Emily was surprised at the offer. Raven wasn't looking directly at her, but was fingering the macramé trim on her tote bag.

"That's good of you. It would save me having to get a boat from the marina."

"No trouble. You could even come swim at our beach if you wanted. I saw that Nate's tearing up your dock this afternoon."

"Oh, that's right. I've probably got a big mess on my shorefront right now."

"We have a float with a springboard."

Emily smiled. "Thanks. I might just take you up on that." Through the front window, she saw Felicia's car pull into her parking space.

"Here's Felicia now. Let's go."

She and Raven rose just as Charlie hung up the phone.

"Hey, ladies, you're not leaving are you?" he called.

"Afraid so." Emily reached for the doorknob.

"Wait. Raven, you didn't even say hi to me."

Charlie jumped up and followed them outside. The heat radiating from the sidewalk smacked them.

"Hi, Charlie," Raven said in sugary sweet tones. "Bye, Charlie."

He frowned. "Come again when you can stay longer."

"Hi, girls!" Felicia climbed out of her car and gathered a briefcase, her camera, and a shopping bag. "You're not leaving me, are you, Emily?"

Emily quashed a stab of guilt. "I typed in all the briefs and the police log. There's an envelope on your desk with Raven's ad copy

245

for an upcoming retreat. We're going for a swim."

"All right. But you've got the school board tonight, right?"

"I'm all over it."

"Great. Thanks."

Emily and Raven ambled toward the marina, chatting like schoolgirls. The dairy bar beside the Heron's Nest had added two new flavors this summer, and Lillian, one of Raven's perennial guests, insisted on riding to the mainland several times a week for a peanut butter fudge cone. Emily laughed and told her how she'd cringed every time anyone set foot on her dock, afraid it would splinter and dump her visitors in the water, giving cause for a lawsuit.

They detoured through the marina store for ice-cold soft drinks, then exited onto the back deck to brave the heat again. Raven's sleek red boat was tied up at one of the marina piers.

They settled into the padded seats, and Emily reached for a life jacket that lay on the deck.

"Do you have another one?"

"Probably. Somewhere in a locker. Go ahead and use that. I hardly ever wear one." Raven started the motor and pulled away with a burst of speed.

"Nice boat," Emily yelled.

"Thanks." Raven pushed the throttle.

Emily couldn't help thinking she'd be home in a fraction of the time it took Nate to deliver her. Of course, on more than one occasion she'd suspected that Nate was deliberately prolonging their ride together.

When they were nearly to the island, Raven eased back on the throttle. "You know, I feel kind of funny advertising that retreat."

"The one with the guru?"

"Yeah. I just . . ." She shrugged and gave a nervous laugh. "I sort of wondered if it's a mistake. You know?"

Emily shook her head. "How do you mean?"

Raven was silent as she concentrated on mooring the boat. When they'd come to a stop, she turned to face Emily. Several Vital Women were approaching the dock to greet them, but Raven lowered her voice and leaned toward her passenger.

"I mean, am I making a huge mistake in promoting beliefs that I've found unsatisfying and empty?"

The desperation in Raven's eyes jarred Emily. She sent up a quick prayer. "Raven, you don't have to feel empty. God can fill that space in your soul."

"Hey, Raven," one of the women called.

Raven glanced up, then whispered, "I have to attend to my guests, but I'll show you where you can change. Can we talk later?"

The pulsing whir of an approaching motorboat drew their attention, and Emily shaded her eyes as she studied the craft.

"That's one of Nate's boats," Raven said.

"Yes, it's the police officers."

"Great. Just what I need." Raven climbed up onto the dock, and Emily joined her.

"Hello, Ms. Miller." Gary Taylor moored the boat and stepped up beside them holding a clipboard, while another uniformed trooper checked the tarp that covered a mound of items in the boat.

"Can I help you?" Raven asked.

"I hope so." Gary lifted the top of the clipboard and reached into the recess beneath. "Detective Blakeney asked me to bring this over and ask if you could identify it."

He brought out a small paper sack that Emily recognized as an evidence bag. Gary unfolded it and tipped the contents into his palm. On shore several women had congregated, but none of them ventured out onto the dock. Emily edged around so that her back was to them, shielding Raven from their eager gazes.

Raven stared at the item in Gary's hand and reached out, slipping the tip of her index finger through the band of the gold ring. She lifted it and turned it, studying the dark stone and raised lettering.

"Where did you get it?"

"It was in the grave we excavated last week. With Joshua Slate's remains."

Raven took a long, slow breath. Her face contorted, and tears welled up in her eyes. Emily stepped closer and slipped her arm around Raven's quaking shoulders.

"Is it yours?" Gary asked.

Raven nodded and wiped her eyes with her hand. "Josh had it. I gave it to him when we were dating. I wore his ring on a chain around my neck."

There was an awkward pause, and Gary asked, "Is there anything else you'd like to tell me about the last time you saw Josh?"

"I . . . don't know anything about his death. I'm sorry."

Gary nodded. "We'll be reopening the file on the party the night Joshua disappeared, Ms. Miller. Detective Blakeney is heading the investigation, and he'll want to talk to you about it."

Raven drew in a ragged breath and blinked, staring toward the trees and the hillside. "All right. I'll be here."

Emily suddenly remembered the list of property owners and party guests she had made. "Gary, I might have something for you." She opened her tote bag. "I photocopied all the old news clippings I could find about that case twelve years ago."

Raven took the opportunity to slip away. She walked up the beach toward the woods, and Emily saw Jenna leave the cluster of women and hurry after her.

"This is great," Gary said, flipping through the folder. "Detective Blakeney will have access to the official case file, of course, but this will give us a feel for the community's perspective back then."

Emily nodded. "Nate and I made a list of all the people attending the party, too. I'm not sure it's complete, but from the memories of people we've talked to and the clippings, this is what we came up with." She ripped the sheet from her notebook. "Oh, and another thing. These are the people who owned land on the island twelve years ago, and this list tells you who owns land now."

Gary eyed her for a moment in silence. Emily wondered if she had overstepped his authority. His prolonged gaze began to rattle her, and she felt a flush sneaking up her neck to her jaw and into her cheeks.

"Say something, Taylor," his partner called

from the boat.

Gary looked down at the papers in his hand, then back at Emily.

"How close are you and Nate?"

"Close enough to go to the town office together and research old tax maps."

"Too close to have dinner with me?"

"Yes."

He nodded. "That's what I thought. Thank you. This should save us a lot of time."

He hopped lightly into the boat, and the other officer started the engine and grinned as Gary cast off. Emily smiled and waved at them, then turned toward shore.

Nate took the boat to the island Tuesday morning between intermittent rain showers. He pulled on his slicker and hopped out of the boat at Emily's new dock. Nice and solid, for a change. If this rain ever quit, he was sure she'd appreciate the large floating sun deck at the end of it. That would be a good selling point, too.

"Well, hi." She smiled up at him as she opened the door. "Nice day for ducks."

"Yes, well, the postmistress reminded me this morning that neither rain nor snow nor sleet . . . etcetera."

She laughed. "Does this mean I have mail?"

He fished a small envelope from the pocket of his slicker. "A letter from your mom."

She tore it open eagerly and smiled as she scanned it. "Sounds like she's doing fine. The planning board approved her remodeling job for the storefront. She expects to have her bookstore open before Labor Day."

"Terrific. Are you busy?"

"Not terribly. The paper comes out today, so we can breathe a little. I think Felicia will want me to do some more typing for her soon, though. She's determined to put out two issues a week and make a go of it."

"Well, I've got mail for the Kimmels, Vital Women, the Derbins, and the boys' camp. Want to tag along?"

She looked past him toward the boat. "I don't have raincoat."

"Grab your jacket. It's dry in the cabin."

She went to get it without further protest, and Nate relaxed, pleased with his success. Emily was a sit-by-the-fireside girl, but she'd agreed to go out and putter around the lake in the rain with him.

The brief ride to the Kimmels' dock barely gave them time to get settled in. The boys were romping in the shallow water, ignoring the raindrops sprinkling down around them. Nate stuffed the mail into the box on the end of the dock and waved to them, then puttered down the shore to the dock at Vital Women. The waterfront was empty, so he tucked the bundle into the large rural mailbox at the end of the pier.

Just the Derbins and Little Cat remained. He wondered if he could talk Emily into returning to the mainland with him for the afternoon. She'd be leaving soon, and he was determined to spend every possible moment in her company.

As he approached the Derbins' dock, Emily laid her warm fingers on his hand. "Let's take Andrew and Pauline's mail up to them."

"All right." He grinned at her and squeezed her hand. Anything to stretch out their time together.

He opened a locker and rummaged until he found his dad's old fishing hat and plopped it atop her golden hair.

"Ready?"

They scrambled up the steps to the dock and ran up the path together, laughing, hand in hand.

Pauli answered their knock on the veranda door.

"Well, hello. I wasn't expecting company."

"Brought you mail." Nate pulled out a circular, the Augusta paper, and two first-class envelopes.

"Come on in," Pauli said. "It's freezing out here."

"We can't —"

Nate swallowed his response. Emily was already through the door and following Pauli through the kitchen to the cabin's living room, where a wood fire blazed in the big fieldstone fireplace.

"Oh, that feels good." Emily stretched her hands toward the fire and smiled at Pauli. "Thanks! I thought I'd freeze in that boat."

Huh. She didn't complain, Nate thought. *And she's only been out there ten minutes.*

"How long are you and Andrew staying here?" Emily asked, and suddenly he realized that she was in the investigative-reporter mode.

"I've got to leave pretty soon," Pauli said. "We're going to have a small memorial for Grandpa in Augusta Saturday, so I think I'll head down Friday. I'm going back to work Monday. Andrew may decide to come up here again after the service."

Pauli stooped and grabbed a slender stick of maple from the wood box and used it to stir up the embers in the fireplace. Then she tossed it onto the coals and added two more sticks to the blaze.

"Say, Pauli . . ." Emily's eyes held a spark of excitement, and Nate peered at her closely.

"What?" Pauli asked, brushing her hands off on her slacks.

Emily looked around, then squared her shoulders. "Don't you have a poker?"

17

Nate paced his mother's kitchen, from the sink to the end of the phone cord that was his tether, which brought him over to where Emily sat on the countertop next to the refrigerator.

"How long should I hold?" he whispered.

"Relax. That means they're patching you through to someone official, not taking a message." She reached up and stroked his cheek, and Nate was tempted to hang up the phone and sweep her into his arms. He leaned toward her, wondering if he could stretch the cord enough to steal a kiss.

At that moment, a deep voice sounded in his ear, and Nate jumped as though he'd been visited by the ghost of Brian Gillespie.

"This is Detective Blakeney. Whattaya got, Holman?"

Nate caught his breath. Emily was laughing silently, and he made a face at her.

"Uh, well, Emily Gray and I just came

from a visit with Pauline Derbin, on Grand Cat. I was delivering her mail."

"Uh-huh."

"Well, sir, Pauline told us her fireplace poker is missing. She's sure her grandfather used to have one, but it's not there. She's been looking for it ever since she arrived at the island last Thursday."

There was a momentary silence, then Blakeney said, "I can't get up there right now, but I'll call the medical examiner's office."

"Yes, sir. Do you suppose he would think that would be a plausible weapon in the Derbin case?"

"I'll ask him. But don't spread this around town. It may be nothing."

"We won't, sir."

"Good work, Holman."

Nate hung up the receiver and swung around to find Emily standing directly behind him. He pulled her in close, and she hugged him.

"He said we did good," Nate whispered in her ear.

"That's a relief. I was afraid he'd be upset to have civilians interfering in his investigation."

"No, he sounded as though he thought it was a promising lead."

"You're talking like them."

"Who?"

"The police."

Nate smiled. "Maybe I'm getting the detective bug again."

"You want to go back to school?"

"I don't know. Maybe." He kissed her lightly. "I think Blakeney's also kicking himself for not noticing that missing poker."

She snuggled in against his chest. "Does your mother need you now?"

"What do have in mind?"

"I think we should go and see Raven."

He tried not to let his disappointment show in his voice, but kissed her temple and whispered, "What for?"

She wriggled from his embrace and picked up her Windbreaker. "Yesterday she asked me if she could talk to me some more about . . . well, about spiritual things. But when Gary showed up and showed her the class ring, it wrecked the mood."

He could see that she was determined, so he reached for his slicker.

"Okay, but we can't mention the poker to anyone. Blakeney's orders."

The door to Raven's office stood open, so Emily rapped softly on the wall as she poked her head in. A woven bamboo shade blew upward in front of the window behind the desk as a cool breeze filtered into the room.

The large office was sparsely furnished, containing just a filing cabinet and a tall, narrow bookshelf besides the desk and chairs. The shelf contained as many colorful stone animal carvings as it did books.

Raven was leaning back in her chair facing the wall, but she looked up when Emily knocked. "Oh, hi."

"Hi. Is this a good time to talk?"

"Sure." Raven started to rise.

"Nate came with me."

He stepped up beside Emily, leaning on the door frame. "Hello, Raven. Do you mind?"

"It's fine by me. Grab a chair." She sat and swiveled her chair so that it faced the desk. "Would you like something to drink? I can ask the cook to bring us some herbal iced tea."

"We're fine," said Emily.

Raven glanced down at the paperwork on her desk. "I was sitting here letting my mind wander. This whole thing about Josh has thrown me on my ear."

Emily and Nate each took one of the wicker chairs and pulled them toward the desk.

Emily glanced at Nate and drew in her

breath. "Raven, I've been praying that the Lord would bring you peace."

"I've had anything but, these last few days. Josh . . . and Henry Derbin. The connection is pretty coincidental, don't you think?" Raven looked at Nate, then back at Emily.

"Do you think Josh's death could have anything to do with Mr. Derbin's murder?" Emily asked.

Raven picked up a stack of papers and shuffled it into a neat pile. "Mr. Derbin's death shocked me as much as it did everyone else."

"What about Josh's death?" Emily asked.

Raven reached for a folder from the top of the file cabinet behind her desk, gathered up the loose papers, and stuffed them inside.

"I keep thinking about it. I suppose the police think that was a murder, too. The state trooper said yesterday they'd want to talk to me about it. I'm not sure I can tell them anything worth hearing."

"Someone buried him up there," Nate said.

"Yes." Raven frowned and clasped her hands on top of the folder.

"What about the kids at the party?" Nate asked. "Do you think some of them might have buried him?"

She shook her head. "His boat was gone

when we left the island. As far as I knew then, all of the kids left. No one saw Josh again that night." Raven tossed her hair and looked toward the wall.

As much as she wanted to ask more questions about the party, Emily knew she should redirect the conversation. *Dear God, please give me wisdom and help me say the right things,* she prayed inwardly. *I believe You brought me here to help Raven, not to talk about Josh's death.*

"Emily." Raven's voice was resolute. "Yesterday we started talking about peace."

"I remember."

"Do you really have inner peace?" Raven asked.

Relief and gratitude warmed Emily. This was God's answer. She was being offered the opportunity to share her faith with Raven again.

Raven turned, and her eyes met Emily's with determination. "You seem so together. Aren't you ever troubled? By anything?"

Emily swallowed. "Sometimes I am," she admitted. "But I know God is in control."

"I keep thinking about Josh and how he went missing. It was bad enough when we all thought he'd drowned, but now . . ." Raven slumped in her chair. "Now I keep going over it in my mind. Like Nate said, someone was involved. Someone knew where his body was all that time. All these years I've tried to tell myself he drowned. There was nothing I could do. But now . . . I keep wondering if his death could have been prevented. Could I have done something that night to change things? Emily, I wish I had the kind of peace you have."

"God can give it to you." Emily offered an encouraging smile.

"I don't know. I've always been such a rebel. As a teenager, I was always questioning authority and testing boundaries. I made fun of the Bible and the Christian kids at school. But secretly, I wondered if they knew something I didn't.'"

Raven pushed her chair back and stood up. She pulled the cord hanging by the window, letting the bamboo shade slide upward. "After years of studying alternative religion and spirituality, I've come to a conclusion. All of that is phony." Her voice broke, and she leaned against the window frame.

"Christ is real, Raven. And you can have real salvation by trusting Him."

Raven turned slowly, her eyelashes lowered. "How can you be so sure?"

Emily got up and went to stand beside her at the window. "He tells us in the Bible.

It's God's Word, and it's true."

Raven nodded slowly.

"Are you ready to trust Him?" Emily asked.

Raven's dark eyes glittered with unshed tears. "I want to."

Two hours later, Detective Blakeney sat down with them in the cozy lounge of the retreat center. Nate seated himself in a chair in one corner, out of Raven's direct line of vision from where she sat with Emily on a loveseat. He'd radioed for the detective after Raven asked Emily to stay with her while she talked to the police. Then he'd met him at the marina dock. Nate felt a little out of place, but Raven had requested that he and Emily stay while she gave her statement, so he made himself as unobtrusive as he could and settled down to listen.

One of Raven's staffers brought in a tray holding several mugs, a coffeepot, and a pitcher of iced pale green liquid. Blakeney accepted a cup of black coffee, as did Nate, and the woman left. The detective sipped his brew, set the mug down, and set up a cassette recorder on the coffee table between him and Raven.

"Ready, Ms. Miller?"

"Yes."

He took out his pen and notebook. "Okay, I'm told you want to make a statement about Joshua Slate's death. Let's get started."

Raven uncrossed her legs, pushing herself farther back into the cushions. "I've been thinking about the night Josh died and trying to remember the details. You know about the party Rocky Vigue threw at his parents' cottage?"

The detective nodded.

"We went together in Josh's dad's boat. After an hour or so at the party, Josh and I took a walk down the shore."

"Why did you do that?" Blakeney asked.

"We wanted to get away from the others."

"You were dating?"

"Yes. We were going steady. I had Josh's class ring, and he had mine. But . . . we'd had some words earlier in the day, and we agreed we wanted to talk in private."

"Which way did you walk?"

"Toward my parents' property," said Raven. "Josh had a flashlight, and we walked along the shore, past the other cottages."

"It's pretty rocky in places."

"Yes."

"How far did you go?"

"Past my folks' place. Almost to where the retreat center's waterfront is now."

"You told the police this twelve years ago."

Raven sat up straighter. "Yes, I did. I showed them the spot where I last saw Josh. It's different, now, though. We had a lot of work done when I built the lodge, and we improved the beach and added a boathouse and docks and a swimming float. None of that was there at the time of the party."

Blakeney took notes while she talked.

Raven went on to relate the details of that night. She and Josh had walked hand in hand down the shore, until they came to the rocky cove where she had last seen him. They climbed up on a big boulder near the shore and sat down.

"And what did you talk about?"

Raven was silent for a moment, then raised her chin. "He told me he wanted to break up."

"Was that unexpected?"

"In a way. But . . . I'd been worried for a few weeks that he was thinking about dating around and wishing he wasn't going steady. I'd heard some rumors. But when he came out and said it with no warning, I was devastated."

"He wanted to see other girls."

"Yes. I . . . started crying. I hoped he would apologize, but he didn't. He got mad instead. So I demanded to know why he wanted to break up. He said he just wasn't happy, but I accused him of lying. I figured he was already seeing someone else behind my back. When he wouldn't admit it, I got angry, too. It got pretty nasty, and we ended up screaming at each other."

"Did the other kids at the party hear you?"

"I don't think so. We were far enough away, and they had music going down near the bonfire."

Blakeney reached for his coffee mug. "Weren't they afraid the people on the mainland would hear the music and see the bonfire?"

Raven's brow wrinkled, and she shook her head. "I don't know. The boys built the fire in a spot where it wouldn't be obvious from shore. It's a mile away, after all. And besides, everybody was drunk by midnight. I think we were all past caring by then."

"But none of the parents knew?"

"Maybe some did, when the kids came home late, but I'm not sure. My folks lived on the edge of town, off the Aswontee Road. They were obliging and didn't wait up for me. They wouldn't have known a thing about it if Josh hadn't . . . disappeared."

Blakeney took a long sip of coffee and picked up his pen again. "So, you and your boyfriend had a loud fight."

"Yes. We stood up on that rock, hollering at each other until I was hoarse. It seems so childish now, but . . . that night it seemed like the end of the world to me. He told me I was selfish for wanting to keep him tied down. I lashed back and told him I'd heard some talk about him and that tramp, Andrea Breyer. He tried to deny it, but after I told him my best friend, Misty, had overheard him bragging to some of the other guys about taking Andrea out, he changed strategy and attacked me. He said I was immature, and the real problem with our relationship was that I was too clingy and possessive. It was like the two years we'd been together meant nothing to him, and he definitely wanted out. His trump card was yelling at me to grow up."

They all sat motionless until Blakeney asked softly, "What happened next?"

Raven reached to lift the pitcher, but her hand shook so badly that Emily took it from her and poured a cupful for her. She set it in front of Raven, but Raven just stared at it.

"That's when he pushed me."

A knot clenched Nate's stomach, and he set his mug down on an end table.

Blakeney cleared his throat. "Ms. Miller, I don't believe I read that in the transcripts of the investigation from twelve years ago."

"No, you didn't. I didn't tell anyone. Well . . . that's not strictly true. But I didn't tell the police. I was afraid." Raven stared at the cup of green tea but didn't touch it.

"He pushed you," Blakeney said.

"Yes. I almost fell off the rock we were standing on. I was furious, and I pushed him back. Hard. He lost his balance and fell over the side."

Nate's throat constricted, and he pulled in a deep breath. He looked across the room at Emily. She was watching Raven's face and stroking her shoulder.

"I was terrified," Raven said, looking Blakeney in the eye. "I yelled, 'Josh?' But he didn't answer. I took off running, back toward the party."

"You didn't check to see if Josh was okay?"

"I was too scared. I didn't know what to do, so I ran. I almost plowed into Andrew, down by the cottage the Kimmels have now."

"Andrew Derbin?" Blakeney asked.

"Yes. He'd helped Rocky set up the party. He said he was coming out to check on me and Josh and see if everything was okay."

"Was he always that conscientious?"

Raven pushed her long hair back over her shoulder. "Andrew always . . . well, I think he liked me back then. You know. He had a crush on me. But I never encouraged him, because I loved Josh." She shook her head. "We were so young. Looking back . . . oh, I don't know. Andrew always hovered, to the point of being annoying. But that night I was glad to see him."

Blakney nodded. "Go ahead."

"Well, Andrew was super that night," Raven said. "At least I thought so at the time. I told him what happened. He sat me down on the Kimmels' dock — it was the Jacksons' then — and told me to wait there while he ran to check on Josh."

"And?"

Raven stood and walked to the window overlooking the beach, keeping her back to the room as she continued.

"He came back a few minutes later and told me Josh was leaving, and I should go back to the party. He said to tell the others that Josh was heading back to the mainland."

Emily was watching Raven, but she turned to look at Nate, and he tried to smile, to let her know everything would be all right. *We'll get through this,* he thought. *It's awful, but Raven needs to do this.* He began to pray inwardly. *Lord, Raven has trusted You today. Give her the courage to finish this. Show her*

269

that what Em said is true, and give her Your peace.

"What was Andrew doing during that time?" Blakeney asked.

Raven turned to face him. "He came back to the beach a few minutes later with some firewood. I don't know if anyone realized how long he'd been gone. By then all the kids were whispering about our fight. I heard one of the guys tell Andrew that Josh had left. We all stayed a little while longer, but Josh's leaving like that put a damper on things. When we all went to the dock to leave, though, I saw that Josh's boat was gone, so I rode home with Misty and her boyfriend."

"Who was her boyfriend?"

"Rand Pooler."

Blakeney scribbled in his notebook. "And you never saw Joshua again?"

"No. The next day it was reported that he never made it home. We kids were . . . well . . . *shocked* doesn't begin to describe it."

"What did you think happened?"

"At first I thought . . . at least, I hoped . . . that it was true Josh had started out for home by himself after we fought. But after awhile I just couldn't make it fit together, unless he was unconscious after he fell."

"Did you ever talk to Andrew Derbin about what happened?"

"I did."

"What did he say happened?"

"He never gave me the details. He was very nice to me after it happened. Everyone was sympathetic, and the kids all came around and tried to support me. But I didn't see Andrew alone for awhile. A week or so after the party, I got up the courage to ask him what he said to Josh that night."

She stopped, and Blakney looked up expectantly. "You need to tell me everything you know, Ms. Miller."

Raven sighed. "Andrew told me, 'Just stick with what you told everyone. Josh was mad. He left. That's it.'"

Nate sipped his cooling coffee, processing what that nonanswer might mean. Raven must have mulled it over many, many times in twelve years.

"Did you ever learn any more?" Blakeney asked.

"No. I thought . . . after a while, I decided he must have been dead when Andrew found him, and I'd killed him. Andrew was trying to protect me from knowing that. I figured Andrew sneaked Josh's boat down the shore and dumped his body in the lake later. But they never found Josh."

"Did you and Andrew Derbin remain friends afterward?" Blakeney asked.

Lines of sorrow etched Raven's youthful face. "We dated a few times that summer, before we went to college. I was horribly depressed, and Andrew was the only one I could be completely honest with."

"But you didn't stay together."

"No. After awhile I realized I didn't really like Andrew very much." Raven walked back to the loveseat and sat down beside Emily. "I started to wonder if he'd really helped me by doing what he did. But we didn't talk about it after that. It was too late to change my story. We both went off to college. Andrew went to the University of Maine. I went to Columbia. We didn't write or anything."

Nate sat forward, wondering if he ought to speak up or not, but Blakeney anticipated his question.

"But you came back to the island," the detective said.

Raven nodded. "I kept thinking about Josh. It was so horrible, and I felt responsible." She looked at Emily apologetically. "It was like he was haunting me. I know now that was irrational, but I thought maybe if I came back here and made myself part of the island where he died, I could find peace. Maybe his spirit would forgive me and leave me alone."

Emily nodded, her face set in compassion. "So you asked your parents if you could use their cottage?"

"Yes, and then Mr. Derbin agreed to sell me the lot next to it. I told him I wanted more land, to make a place where people could come and find peace. I guess he liked that idea, because he sold me six lots, and I got the shoreline down past where Josh fell off the rock."

"But you didn't know he was buried up on the hill?" Blakney asked.

Raven shook her head. "No. All I can figure now is . . . Andrew must have done that after the party."

18

"Out of here, Holman! She's working." Felicia scowled at Nate as he stood in the doorway to the newspaper office.

"Aw, come on, Felicia. I just came over to see if Emily could take a late lunch with me."

Emily looked up at him from behind the computer monitor on Charlie Benton's desk. He had looked like that in high school, when his father asked him who drank the last root beer in the cooler. Innocent expression, faded Maine Black Bears T-shirt, frayed cutoffs, size thirteen sneakers. His dark hair peeked out from under a Red Sox cap, and his brown eyes held a glint of laughter.

She smiled at the memories his appearance evoked. "I'm famished."

"Great. I was afraid you'd already eaten. Where's Charlie?"

"Out selling ads," Felicia said. "All right,

Nate, I'll let her go with you, but only because she's been working all morning. But don't you keep her away from here long. We have to get the weekend edition to the printer tomorrow morning, and she's writing a very important story."

"About what?"

"The divers."

Nate nodded. "I didn't realize you interviewed them, Emily. They launched their boat full of equipment from the marina pier this morning."

"Yeah, I think you were making your mail run when I talked to the warden supervisor heading it up." She rose and reached for her tote bag.

"Have they found anything?"

"Nothing useful." Emily turned to look at Felicia. "Want to come with us?"

"Thanks, but I had a burger on my way here from interviewing Detective Blakeney. Besides, I'm expecting a call."

Nate guided Emily outside. The heat was pleasant today, not oppressive. She took sunglasses from her bag and slipped them on. "Where are we eating?"

"How about my mom's kitchen? Or would you rather eat out?"

"No, let's save money."

He grinned and took her hand. "Good.

More privacy that way."

She looked toward the water. Between the thrift shop and the Lumberjack restaurant, she could see an expanse of the glittering lake. "The wardens say it's a long shot they'll find anything significant in the water."

"Yeah," he agreed. "There's too much of it. Water, that is."

She nodded. "It's too deep and . . . just too big. Especially when you're looking for something as small as a poker."

"I expect they started looking near Derbin's shore?"

"Yes. Then they moved out away from the dock toward Baxter."

"It must be a hundred feet deep out there." Nate stopped and gazed out toward the island.

"Deeper. But it looks like they're still at it."

Nate shook his head and resumed walking toward his house. "It's the perfect place to dump something made of wrought iron."

"Felicia talked to the state police spokesman this morning," Emily said. "They need the poker to be sure, but the medical examiner says the impressions on Mr. Derbin's head are consistent with that being the murder weapon."

"Wow. You said that without even wincing."

She scrunched up her face at him. "I know. You have to stay detached to cover something like this."

"I guess cops have to do that, too — separate their feelings from their job."

"I guess so."

"That's something I'd have to work on if I decided to go that direction after all."

"You're seriously thinking about it?"

"Well . . . yeah."

The rush of excitement she felt for him surprised Emily. If Nate could realize his dream after all these years, it would change his outlook on a lot of things, she was sure. But it would complicate his future, too. Would it affect hers? She couldn't help wondering.

"Keep me posted," she said.

Connie had set the table for two and left salad and a dish of leftover lasagna in the refrigerator for them. While their plates were heating in the microwave, Emily filled their glasses with ice water.

"Felicia talked to Detective Blakeney this morning, too," she said.

Nate brought the salad dressing from the refrigerator — blue cheese for himself and low-calorie French for Emily. "I saw the boat he's using at the boys' camp dock this morning. What's he up to? Interviewing all the party survivors?"

"Yeah, he's been interviewing all the people on the list we made who still live around here. He told Felicia he's even called some of the ones who've moved away."

"So, he was talking to Rand Pooler this morning?"

"Guess so. But Rand was tied up at the camp the day Mr. Derbin was killed. It was the end of their first week of camp, and a new batch of boys was coming in."

They continued to discuss the case while enjoying their meal then moved out to the marina's back deck and, for a few minutes, stood watching the boats anchored between Baxter and Grand Cat.

"They'll never find it," Nate said.

"Probably not." Emily shrugged. "Nothing we can do."

He stooped and kissed her lightly. "Can I see you later?"

"I was hoping you'd take me home."

The back door of the store opened, and Allison Woods looked out at them. "Oh, good, Nate, you're here! A gentleman is arriving at five o'clock, and he needs transportation to Little Cat. He's the headliner at the boys' campfire tonight."

Nate lowered his eyebrows. "Guest speakers for the kiddy campers now?"

"He's a magician."

Emily grabbed his wrist. "Let me go with you. Maybe we can see the show."

Nate laughed. "You're easy to please, aren't you?"

"I love magicians."

"All right, be back here at five."

When she got back to the newspaper office, Felicia jumped up from her chair. "I'm so glad you're back! You've got to go to Bangor."

"Bangor?"

"Yes. Rocky's cut a deal with the district attorney, and his lawyer has agreed to give us a story."

"Then you should go."

"No, Rocky insisted on talking to you."

Emily stared at her. "Why me?"

"He thinks you're the greatest, I guess. You work for a big-time paper." Felicia didn't quite meet Emily's gaze.

"I'm sorry. You're a very good reporter, Felicia."

"Don't sweat it. At least it's the *Journal* he's giving his exclusive interview to. The basics are likely to be on the TV news tonight, but I'm hoping Rocky will tell you some details they don't release to the rest of the media. After all, we're the local press in his hometown. Even though he's in big trouble, he wants the attention back home. Make sure you get a decent picture."

Emily grabbed a new reporter's notebook and accepted the digital camera Felicia thrust into her hands. "Did the lawyer say what the deal is? I mean, he's already confessed. What else can he possibly give them?"

"In exchange for a suspended sentence and probation for his thefts, Rocky's going to tell them about the party when Joshua Slate died."

Emily swallowed hard. "You mean . . . Rocky is implying he knows something about Josh's death?"

"I don't know for sure. Just get down there. It will take you an hour to get to the jail. Do you know where it is?"

"I think so. Penobscot County Jail, right?"

Felicia rattled off a string of streets and landmarks, and Emily nodded.

"Okay. And call Nate, would you? Tell him I'll try to be back at five, but if I'm not there to just go without me."

"You've got to write the story when you get home. The proofs go to the printer in the morning. I'll be rearranging the front page while you're gone."

Emily winced and gave a little moan. "All right, but I really wanted to write a nice, upbeat feature about that magician." She glanced at her watch. Nearly two o'clock. As she turned toward the door, she knew her time with Nate that evening would be minimal.

"Wait." Felicia pulled out her cell phone and rummaged in a drawer, coming up with a headset. "Take this and call me when you leave the interview. It's a hands-free headset. You can talk to me on the way back and dictate your story."

Emily grinned. "Terrific. But call Nate for me now."

Emily hurried into the marina at five minutes past five carrying Felicia's camera and her tote bag. Nate was in the store greeting a thin man with wispy white hair and a teenaged boy.

"Emily!" he cried. "I was afraid you wouldn't get back in time. This is Mr. Blanchard, otherwise known as the Great Blanchini. And his assistant, Michael."

"My grandson," the old man said with a sweet smile.

"It's a pleasure to meet you, sir."

Emily shook his hand, then Michael's, and

followed them and Nate out to the dock. Nate and Michael loaded two large, black suitcases into the cabin cruiser. By the time they disembarked at Little Cat, she had learned to make a quarter disappear and pull a string of knotted handkerchiefs from her closed fist. She had also extracted enough background information from Blanchard for a feature in the weekend's *Journal.*

Rand Pooler and his head counselor met them at the dock, and Rand let the counselor lead Blanchard and Michael off to prepare for their presentation.

"Nate," Rand said as soon as the others were out of earshot, "aren't you related to one of the cops who was here this morning?"

"Gary Taylor's my cousin," Nate said. "He's a state trooper."

"He's the one. If you see him in the near future, could you tell him I learned something else after they left here that might interest them?"

"Sure."

Emily's fascination with the gentle old magician fled from her mind. She stepped closer and gave the camp director her full attention.

"What's up?" Nate asked.

"Well, on Saturday — that is, the Saturday

Henry Derbin was killed —"

Nate nodded.

"We had a few campers staying over the weekend. Most of the boys from the first week of camp went home that morning, but we had seven who were staying another week. On Saturdays, we try to have a special outing that gets the stay-over campers out of the way and gives them a treat the others don't get."

"Do you mind?" Emily asked, bringing out her notebook and pen.

"I guess not," Rand said. "But tell the cops before you put it in print."

"We will," Nate promised.

"And you can't use the boys' names."

"I wouldn't do that," Emily said.

"Okay. I don't know why this didn't get back to me, but I guess the guys didn't think it was important. Two of our senior counselors took the seven stay-overs down the lake for an overnight canoe trip. They left early Saturday, about eight in the morning. We wanted them to get away before the new arrivals started coming."

"So . . . they canoed south?" Nate asked. "Right past Grand Cat?"

"That's right. Jeff Lewis offered to let them land on the beach at his lodge and hike off to a campsite he's made back in the woods. He has a lot more property than we do on this island, and every summer he lets our boys take a few outings on his land. In return, I recommend his lodge to any parents who want to stay overnight in the area. It's good for both businesses."

Emily's pulse quickened. Rand was about to tell them something important. She was sure of it.

"So, anyway, it may be nothing, but . . . well, we've got this little guy named Sherman." Rand looked over his shoulder toward the shore, where Emily could see the boys forming lines in front of the lodge. "He's here for the summer. I wouldn't say his parents dumped him exactly, but he's here for eight weeks. For a nine-year-old, that's a long time."

"I'll say." Nate looked nearly as forlorn as poor little Sherman must have felt when his parents left him on the island.

"He's a good kid," Rand said. "Kind of a nerd, though. He's not as big as the other boys his age, and he's bookish. His favorite possession is a set of high-powered binoculars. The kid wears them everywhere. In fact, I told him he ought to leave them here when they went on the overnight. I was afraid he'd lose them or break them. But he insisted he'd be careful, and the counselor in charge said he'd keep an eye on him."

"Did Sherman see something in particular with those binocs?" Nate asked.

Rand pointed toward the shore of Grand Cat, across a half mile of open water. "I was really busy that day, and I didn't see it, but Sherman says they saw a canoe put out from the dock over there."

Emily said at once, "Henry Derbin's dock."

"Right. Like I said, apparently it didn't click with the counselors in the war canoe that it was important. But I like to get to know the boys, and I take turns eating with the different cabins. This noon I sat with Sherman's cabin, and he started asking me about the murders on Grand Cat. I don't know how these little guys heard so much about what's been going on."

Nate grinned. "Probably some junior counselor told it like a ghost story."

"Could be. The skeleton on top of the hill would be a good campfire tale, I guess. However he learned about it, Sherman also knew about Mr. Derbin's murder. And he says to me, 'I'll bet that guy in the red canoe had something to do with it.' "

19

"Sherman saw a man in a red canoe leaving the dock?" Emily wrote down the details in her notebook.

Rand nodded. "I had no idea what he was talking about. So he told me his story, and afterward I called the two counselors that went on the canoe trip in to my office and asked them about it. They agreed they'd seen a man in a canoe leaving Derbin's that morning."

"Did he go to the marina?" Nate asked. "I didn't rent any canoes that early."

Rand shook his head. "They don't know where he went, but they said he was heading north, toward Turtle Island and the campground on Whitney Point. That general direction."

Nate nodded. "We'll tell the officers. I expect I'll see some of them tonight."

"Maybe we'd better not stay for the magic show." Emily hated to give it up, but Rand's information sounded valuable.

"We're going to start right away," Rand said. "The boys will have their supper first — a weenie roast. Then the show."

"Let's stay," Nate said, and Emily couldn't hold back her grin.

"Thanks! I haven't eaten a hot dog roasted over a wood fire for years."

Nate grabbed her hand as they followed Rand to the outdoor campfire area on a rise overlooking the waterfront. Emily spotted the table set up by the kitchen staff.

"Oh, Nate, look! S'mores! I want to come to camp here."

He laughed and steered her toward the end of the line of campers.

A half hour later the counselors herded the sticky-faced boys onto the rough benches forming a semicircle facing the fire pit. Nate handed Emily a damp cloth he'd begged from the cook.

"Wash your hands, babe."

"I wouldn't talk if I were you." She reached up and scrubbed a bit of marshmallow from his upper lip.

Nate bent toward her, but she leaned back. "Uh-uh. There are children watching."

Rand stepped forward and calmed the boys then announced, "I give you now, the

Great Blanchini!"

The boys whooped and cheered as Blanchard entered from behind a storage shed, his black cape swirling, then tapped his wand on the rustic podium, sending off a spray of colored sparks.

Emily forgot to take notes as she watched the show, enthralled with the older man's graceful movements and delightful surprises.

"And now I will have my assistant, Michael the Magnificent, help me with my famous mind-reading trick."

Blanchini handed his tall black hat to his grandson, and Michael, in black pants and glittering gold shirt, walked around the crescent of benches holding the hat in front of the boys.

"Now, each of you boys just reach in your pockets and pull out whatever you have there and put it in the hat," Blanchini said. "Michael the Magnificent will then hold up the items behind me, where I cannot see them, and I will tell you what they are."

The boys protested loudly, and Blanchini waved his wand at them.

"You doubt my capabilities? I will show you! We use no mirrors, no tricks. But when Michael the Magnificent holds up the item and concentrates on it, I will receive a message from his brain and tell you what item he is holding. And I assure you, we will return all belongings to the owners when we are done."

The boys began digging out trinkets. When Michael came to them, Nate dropped a quarter in the hat, and Emily added her cell phone.

"That ought to shake him up," Nate laughed.

"Not the Great Blanchini," Michael assured them. "Grandpa's very good at this."

He walked to the front and stood behind his grandfather, then reached into the hat.

"Are you ready, O Great Blanchini?"

The magician, now seated on a camp stool, nodded. "Proceed, Assistant."

"The first item." Michael held up a comb. "We'll start with an easy one."

Blanchini sat silently for a moment, then smiled. "A comb."

The boys shouted and clapped.

When they were quiet again, Michael laid the comb aside and reached into the hat again. "All right, next item. O, Great Blanchini! This is something you'll really like."

"Let me see." The magician squared his shoulders and stared off into the sky behind the boys. "It's something round. It has a round . . . a round dial. It must be a compass."

The boys erupted once more in cheers.

The Great Blanchini held up his hands.

"Thank you! Next item, please, Michael the Magnificent."

The old man went through a dozen turns, revealing each trinket, including Emily's phone. Near the end of the performance, a boy dashed up to Michael and slipped something into the hat.

"Oh, man," Michael said, staring down into it. "Great Blanchini, I'm not sure I can hold this one. It's . . . well, it's something you don't see often."

Blanchini pondered for a long moment. "Aha. I perceive . . . it is a living creature."

"Yes!" cried the boy who had donated it.

"Is it a worm?"

Michael's head drooped. "I'm sorry, Great One. That is not correct. It is a salamander."

Amid howls of laughter, Michael carried the hat back to the prankster and let the boy retrieve his pet.

"And finally . . ." Michael held up a dark square object as big as his palm. "O, Blanchini, think very hard. Can you see what I am thinking?"

The magician cleared his throat and shifted. "It's . . . very difficult. Is this an exotic object?"

"No, no, it's actually quite common, though perhaps not in a boys' camp. Just think hard, Great One."

Blanchini sat for a moment in a pensive pose, then raised his chin.

"It's a wallet."

The boys screamed and clapped so loudly that Emily covered her ears with her hands.

"Yes, it is," Michael said. "And since it feels rather thick, I'd better return it immediately to its owner."

He flipped open the billfold and squinted at something inside it. "Ah. This wallet belongs to . . ."

The boys waited in silence.

"Henry Derbin!"

In Nate's boat once more, Emily sat down, exhausted.

"Long day," Nate said.

"I'll say. Felicia wants me to go back and put some finishing touches on the story about Rocky. I told her I would, after the magic show. I might as well go now, while you talk to the cops."

Nate shoved off from the dock and started the engine. They'd left Blanchard and Michael at the camp to finish the show, with Rand promising to deliver them to the mainland after the magician had packed up his paraphernalia. Emily was glad. It meant they had some privacy. Nate kept the boat moving with the motor idling along quietly enough that they could talk.

"What a stunning trick the Great Blanchini's pulled," she said.

Nate nodded. "Incredible."

"Seems those little campers get around."

"Yeah," Nate said. "Two Saturdays ago they canoed south and saw someone leaving Derbin's dock, and last Saturday they canoed north and had their outing at the Whitney Point campground and one of them picked up Henry Derbin's wallet."

Emily reached into her tote bag and pulled out the plastic zipper bag that now contained the wallet. "Can you believe that boy didn't tell his counselor when he found it?"

"I'll believe anything coming out of Little Cat now."

She tucked the plastic bag back into the tote and snapped the closure to secure it.

"So, what happened in Bangor today?" Nate asked.

"They gave me twenty minutes with Rocky and his lawyer. The lawyer kept telling him to be careful what he made public, but Rocky seemed to want to talk."

"And he picked you to spill it to."

She shrugged. "Well, he'd already given the police his statement. But apparently this was part of the deal. He named me as the reporter he wanted to speak to. That floors me."

"You're good, Emily. Everyone knows that."

"Aw, that's a silly rumor."

"Is not. I went online and took a gander at the Web site for the newspaper in Hartford. You have to be good to byline in that rag."

She felt her cheeks flush. "Quit it."

Nate smiled "I'm just proud of you. What did Rocky have to say?"

"He said he'd told the police that after the infamous keg party, Andrew took him into his confidence. The other guests left, and they stayed behind to clean up."

Nate's eyes narrowed. "Couldn't leave any evidence for Marvin and Truly to find the next morning."

"Right. He'd have been grounded for a month. But that's not all they did."

"Are you going to tell me?"

"He said they were both hammered, but Andrew took him down the shore to where Josh had fallen on the rocks, and Josh was dead."

Nate caught his breath. "I guess I expected

something like that, but even so, it's stupefying."

"Yeah. Rocky said he sobered up in a hurry."

"Pretty gruesome for a couple of eighteen-year-olds to deal with."

Emily nodded. "Andrew must have given it some thought. He didn't want to take a chance the body would surface, so instead of putting him in the lake —"

"Where everyone would look," Nate cut in.

"Yeah, exactly. Rocky said they managed to carry Josh's body up to the hill and bury him."

"They did a good job, I guess. No one found the spot for twelve years."

"The fact that Henry Derbin kept everyone off his land helped," Emily said.

"No doubt."

"And Rocky said he mentioned it once to Andrew, later that summer, suggesting they go up there and make sure the grave was well concealed. But Andrew said not to. Nobody ever went up there, and if they did, there would be a bigger chance that someone would see them and find out about Josh. So they just stayed away from the grave."

Nate's eyebrows drew together, and he

shook his head. "All these years."

"That's right. All these years, Rocky has never gone back up that hill."

"I'm surprised he told you all that." Nate glanced over at her.

"Me, too, and that his lawyer let him. I think the lawyer wants some publicity."

"But they never release information like that before the trial!"

"Well, Rocky's case isn't going to trial. He'll appear in court, and the judge will sentence him for the thefts. Jail sentence with most of it suspended, maybe a fine, and some restitution. But most of the loot will go back to the owners."

Nate whistled softly. "What does this mean for Andrew?"

She looked back toward the islands. The sun was sinking behind Grand Cat. "No idea. I suspect Blakeney will grill him again."

"Those guys lied about everything."

"Well, yes. Don't take it so hard, sweetie." She reached over and squeezed his hand. "They've been lying about it for twelve years. They weren't about to change their story now, just because I stumbled on the grave. Think about it. They *had* to keep lying."

"They must have been terrified when they

heard you'd found it." Nate pointed across the water toward two more boats heading for Baxter. "Looks like they've called off the search for the day. The divers are packed up to leave."

"Maybe we can catch Gary or Blakeney at the dock."

"Andrew's likely to lose his job at the statehouse over this."

"I suppose so," Emily said.

"Sure. The governor won't want him around after this scandal breaks." Nate throttled back the speed even more and reached for her hand. "Let's pray before we talk to the police."

20

The shore by the boat dock on Little Cat teemed with campers in swim trunks when Nate and Gary arrived Friday morning. The counselor in the lifeguard's chair on the second dock, near the shallow, buoyed area for nonswimmers, waved to them. Intrigued by the arrival of a uniformed officer on the island, the boys watched the men as they took the path up the beach toward the director's office.

"Where's Blakeney today?" Nate asked his cousin.

"He's tied up in court. Told me to come interview the boys. We don't want to sit on this."

"No," Nate agreed. "The boy who found the wallet is going home to New Jersey Saturday."

Rand Pooler met them on the porch of the office cabin.

"Hi. I've got Sherman here, and while you

talk to him, I'll send down to the waterfront for Caden, the boy who found the wallet last weekend."

"Thanks." Gary turned toward the porch swing where Sherman waited. Nate leaned against one of the posts holding up the porch roof and let Rand make the introduction.

The boy swung his bare legs back and forth as they dangled over the edge of the swing, not quite reaching the floor. The famous pair of binoculars hung around his neck, as did a silver whistle on a lanyard braided from strands of red and purple gimp.

"Officer, this is Sherman McGraw," Rand said.

Sherman looked up briefly at the camp director and the policeman, but didn't say anything.

"Howdy," said Gary. "I'm Trooper Taylor."

Sherman pulled one skinny leg up onto the swing to investigate the scab on his knee.

"I thought you might want him to walk down to the waterfront with you afterward and point out where he saw the canoe," said Rand.

Gary squatted so that his face was on the boy's eye level. "Okay, Sherman, would you tell me your story?"

Rand left them, and Nate stood leaning against the post and watching. He didn't want to make the boy nervous, although he didn't think, from the look of him, that there was much that would faze Sherman. His face didn't seem capable of expression aside from the occasional eyebrow twitch.

"Well, my whole canoe saw the guy," Sherman started. "But I'm the one with the binoculars, so I got a close-up view of him."

"What did he look like?" Gary asked.

"Old."

"How old?"

"As old as you."

Nate couldn't help grinning, and noted that Gary was struggling to conceal a smile as well.

"Can you tell me what color his hair was?"

"Mmm . . . brown, I guess. Or blond. But he wasn't wearing his life jacket, I know that for sure. He was breaking the law, wasn't he?"

"Well, he may have had it in the canoe with him. Grown-ups do that sometimes, and the law allows it."

Sherman scowled. "Well, Uncle Don told us we have to wear ours anytime we're in a boat. He said it's a law."

"Well, it's different for you kids here at

the camp."

"Huh."

Gary shifted his weight. "What else do you remember, Sherman?"

"I saw him dump something over the side."

Gary looked up sharply. "Could you see what it was?"

Sherman shook his head. "Nobody else believed me, but I saw it. He dropped something in the water, and it made a little splash."

"Did you know about the wallet, too?" Gary asked.

"Not until right before the magic show. But Caden's not in my cabin."

"Were you on the outing last Saturday when he found it?"

"Yeah, but I didn't know about him finding it. I think he hid it for awhile, or maybe he showed the guys in his cabin. Last night some of the guys were saying that if he didn't turn it in, they'd tell Uncle Jason."

"Is that why he put it in the magician's hat?"

Sherman shrugged. "Maybe. So they couldn't say he stole it. Or maybe just to show off, I don't know."

Gary put his hand on Sherman's shoulder. "I think that's a very good theory. You're not only observant, you're a good thinker."

"Thanks."

Nate followed Gary and Sherman down to the shore and around the corner of a little cove. He wondered if he should ask Rand to let them take the boy out in his boat for a few minutes.

Sherman stepped with one foot on a rock that protruded out of the water. He pointed. "That's about where I spotted the canoe." He raised his binoculars to his eyes.

"Right out there between here and Grand Cat?" Gary asked.

"Uh-huh. He came from that house over there. At least, he came from their dock. And then he paddled down past our island, thataway." Sherman turned and pointed north.

Gary turned to Nate. "After I talk to Caden, do you mind taking me to the campground?"

"Not at all."

"Hey, thanks for your help, Sherman."

Sherman lowered his binoculars. He nodded at Gary, almost smiling.

As they started for the campground, Nate kept thinking about the suspects in the Derbin murder. He and Emily had boiled their list down to Raven, Andrew, and

Rocky. The canoeist had been a man, and anyway Raven had more than likely spilled everything she knew. After the arrest, Rocky also seemed to be coming clean. Andrew was really the only one who didn't seem to know anything. But he still denied any involvement.

"That nature club thing is closing, huh?" said Gary.

"What?" Nate realized he was referring to Raven's retreat. "Oh, Vital Women? I don't know. Raven's had some major changes in her philosophy, but I hadn't heard that she was closing the retreat center. Did you hear something?"

"Just a rumor, I guess. One of the cottagers on Grand Cat mentioned it."

The usual gossip, Nate thought. "I wouldn't put much stock in it. Say, the police don't think Josh died from falling off that rock, do they?"

Gary squinted against the sunlight. "How did you find out about that?" His pursed lips indicated curiosity, but not surprise. More like chagrin that Nate knew where their investigation was leading.

"Emily said the medical examiner's office released the autopsy report."

"Should have known."

Nate grinned. "Yeah, she stayed late to

302

work on her story last night, and she heard. She said the report shows that Josh suffered multiple head wounds, and the ME doesn't think a fall from the rocks caused them all."

"Right, but I'm not supposed to talk about it."

"What about the wallet?" Nate asked. "Can you talk about that?"

"What are you doing, getting information to feed to Emily for the paper?"

"No, but I was thinking. The day Andrew came, he told me they couldn't find his grandfather's wallet. Like maybe it was a robbery, you know? Then, a few days later, some kid picks that wallet up out of the grass at the campground. No cash or credit cards in it, but it still had Henry's driver's license, his medical cards, pictures of the grandkids, all that kind of stuff. It was almost" — Nate eyed him, a bit hesitant to voice the thought, but decided to put it out there — "almost like whoever took it wanted it to be found."

Gary took his sunglasses from his pocket and slid them on. "I hear you."

When they arrived at the campground at Whitney Point, they found a sign on the office door that said OUT, BE BACK SOON.

"Well, how long is soon?" Gary rolled his eyes.

Nate elbowed him. "Not long." He pointed toward the trees beyond the row of small cabins.

Gretchen Langdon Barrett was emerging from the woods, where a path meandered among the campsites by the lake. She had been in Raven's class, but looked younger than her thirty years with her ginger-colored hair in pigtails and a lithe figure shown off in khaki shorts and a blue tank top. Her face tightened as she spotted Gary in his uniform.

"Hi, Nate. Hi, Gary. Is something wrong?"

"Well, no," said Gary. "I'd just like to ask you a couple of questions. A couple of Saturdays ago — the day Henry Derbin was killed, to be exact — some of the boys at Camp Dirigo say they saw a man in a canoe leave the Derbins' dock and head down toward this end of the lake. I was wondering if you know of anyone here taking a canoe out that morning."

Gretchen shook her head slowly. "Our guests bring kayaks and canoes, or they can borrow our canoes and boats, and they can go out anytime they want. Of course, we weren't full to capacity that weekend. We're just getting to that point now. But still . . . I don't think I recall anyone specifically taking a canoe out that day."

"This is very important," said Gary. "It could make a huge difference."

"You could ask my husband. Joe went to Bangor this morning, but he might remember something." Gretchen's thin lips formed a frown. "Is this about Mr. Derbin's murder? I don't know anything about it."

"Do you keep records of who takes out the canoes that belong to you?"

"We have a sign-out sheet, but we don't keep it. I usually toss it at the end of the day. That's almost two weeks ago you're talking about."

"Well, if you didn't see anything, you didn't see anything," said Gary. "But I would also like to talk to you about the party on Grand Cat the night after your high school graduation twelve years ago."

Nate thought he saw Gretchen flinch a little. He figured it was still a touchy subject for most of the people who'd been at the party, and the discovery of Josh's remains had stirred up a lot of feelings they'd never expected to face again.

"Yeah, okay. I was there." She lowered her eyes, working her jaw a little. Her voice was thick, as though she might begin to cry. "What do you want to know?"

"What can you tell me about Raven and Josh's walk that night?" Gary asked. "Did you notice them leave the party?"

"Sure, I remember that." Gretchen crossed her arms, turning her gaze toward the water. "They went off alone for awhile, then Raven came back by herself. And Andrew seemed to be gone awhile, which I thought was odd since he had a crush on Raven, and never seemed to let her out of his sight."

"How was Raven when she came back?" Gary asked.

"She was upset. But she told everyone she and Josh had a spat. I think he dumped her that night. I don't know why she cared that much, though. She could have any guy she wanted. Andrew was crazy about her."

Nate thought he detected a note of bitterness in her voice.

Gary said, "Do you think there was something between Raven and Andrew?"

"Not really. Raven never paid him any attention until Josh disappeared." Gretchen bit her lip. "I was kind of jealous of her, 'cause I liked Andrew at the time. I'd been trying to get him to notice me all year. Girls with freckles and braces don't get much notice in high school." She let out a nervous laugh.

Gary nodded. "Did you ever date Andrew Derbin?"

She shook her head. "No. I decided he wasn't worth it. I went away to college that fall, and I started dating other guys. Andrew became less important in a hurry."

Gary scribbled something down on his notepad then looked up. "Gretchen, I have several witnesses claiming a canoe came down here toward your campground beach the morning Mr. Derbin was killed. Was Andrew Derbin here at all that day?"

She drew herself up, breathing deeply, and her face went red.

"I guess it's kind of foolish to protect him," she said. "If he had something to do with his grandfather's death. Or Josh's."

"Just tell the truth," said Gary.

Nate held his breath.

"Yeah, okay. I saw someone pull in with a vehicle I didn't recognize as one of my campers. There was a red canoe on top. I was in the office, and I watched him unload the canoe. It looked like Andrew. I thought it was probably him, and I was going to go out and speak to him, but I didn't get a chance. I got a call right then from someone wanting to make a reservation. But whoever it was launched the canoe from my waterfront. Later that morning I drove over to the bank in Baxter, and when I came back the SUV was gone. I was kicking myself because I'd missed him."

Gary took down the statement. "So you're not one hundred percent sure it was Andrew Derbin?"

She hesitated. "It was him."

Gary eyed her for a moment, and she flushed.

"Why didn't you just tell me that before?"

Gretchen pulled in a deep breath. "Look, Joe never liked Andrew, okay? My husband is a great guy, but he has a teeny little jealous streak. He knows I used to have a crush on Andrew. It doesn't matter to him that it was more than a decade ago. Whenever Joe hears that Andrew is in town, he gets edgy. So I didn't tell him." She shrugged and met Gary's gaze. "Look, I didn't talk to Andrew that day. But it was him. Now, if you don't have to, could you please not tell anyone?"

Gary made another notation on his pad. "You have to understand, Gretchen, if this goes anywhere, you could be called to testify."

She sighed, then nodded. "All right. If it's necessary."

Gary smiled. "You're doing the right thing."

When they reached the dock, Gary said to Nate, "Could I ask you for one more favor?"

"Grand Cat?" Nate asked.

"Yep. I'll be taking Andrew in for questioning."

21

That afternoon the door to the *Baxter Journal*'s office flung open, banging against the wall, and Nate charged in.

"The divers found the poker!"

"You're joking." Felicia stared at him.

"No, I'm not. It was thirty feet down, in the muck and weeds."

"Where?" Emily seized the camera bag from its spot on the shelf of telephone books.

"A hundred yards off Henry Derbin's dock, in a direct line between the cottage and the campground beach."

"Go!" Felicia cried. "I'll stay by the phone."

Emily dashed out the door and ran toward the marina. When she arrived, panting, in the parking lot, Nate caught up with her.

"Felicia says to ask if they're going to charge Andrew now."

Emily fumbled with the clasp on the

camera bag, keeping one eye on the knot of officers crowding around three squad cars and a Warden Service pickup.

"Did you see Blakeney?" she asked.

"I was in the boat with him when the divers pulled up the poker and handed it to him."

She flashed him an apologetic smile. "Guess I'll have to interview you later. You don't mind, do you?"

"I'm getting used to it. Great way to end your vacation, huh?"

She frowned and avoided his piercing gaze. She'd tried not to think much about the end of this interlude, and for the most part she'd stayed busy enough to keep her thoughts under control. She had a sudden longing to talk to her mother.

When this is over. I'll call Mom as soon as I get the details from Blakeney.

"Where's Blakeney now?"

"He took Gary and two other men out to the island in the Warden Service boat."

"Should I go out there?"

"I don't think you need to."

The half dozen officers in the parking lot began walking toward the dock, and Emily looked out past them. A boat was cruising in to dock.

"Thanks, Nate." She gulped in air, trying

311

in vain to calm the nerves that always kicked up in a situation like this, and strode past the side of the store, onto the dock.

The officers let her pass them and click pictures as Gary climbed out of the boat and turned to steady Andrew. Blakeney waited in the boat below Andrew as he climbed to the dock. He wobbled on the step, his hands handcuffed behind him, and Blakeney and Gary both reached to grasp the prisoner's arms.

Emily hated the picture she saw through her viewfinder, but she clicked.

Gary and two other troopers guided Andrew past her toward the parking lot, and Emily's heart wrenched as she observed the bitter set to Andrew's lips. He raised his chin and met her eyes for an instant, but said nothing.

"Detective Blakeney!" Emily rushed toward him as he left the boat, determined to get the story quickly. "Have you charged Andrew Derbin with his grandfather's death?"

Blakeney frowned at her as he gained his footing beside her on the pier. "I'm surprised you weren't at his house when we put the cuffs on, young lady."

Emily gave him a regretful smile. She didn't like it when public servants looked on her as a pest.

"The answer is yes." Blakeney took his hat off, wiped his forehead on his sleeve, and replaced the hat. "We've charged him with two counts of murder."

"Two?" Emily's heart raced.

"That's right. Henry Derbin and Joshua Slate."

She jotted notes as she talked. "Can you make a case in the Slate murder?"

"That's for the prosecutor to decide. That's all I'll say on that for now, but I expect it to go to court."

"And the Henry Derbin killing?"

Blakeney's shoulders relaxed. "We found a blunt instrument this afternoon."

"The poker."

"Did I say that?"

"I saw one of your men putting it in a car over there." She pointed toward the parking lot. "Pauli Derbin told me two days ago that her grandfather's poker was missing, and a boy at Camp Dirigo said he saw a man in a canoe drop something in the water the day Henry Derbin was killed, in the area where you found that poker."

Blakeney smiled. "You're a smart cookie, aren't you? Well, keep in mind when you write your story that we haven't established yet whether that poker is the murder weapon in the Derbin case. I'll tell you this: Pauline Derbin has identified it as an item from her grandfather's cottage, but the medical examiner will have to tell us whether it was used in the homicide. Have you got that clear?"

Emily felt a flush sting her cheeks, but she continued to look him in the eye. "Yes, sir. What else can you tell me?"

He fished in his breast pocket and handed her his business card. "Call me later, Miss Gray. Give me at least two hours."

"All right, but can you tell me —"

"Two hours." Blakeney walked to his car and drove away.

Emily swallowed and looked up to find Nate standing beside her. "Guess he told me."

"Go with me to bring Pauli and her luggage to shore?" Nate put on his best begging-puppy expression as Emily opened the door of her cottage.

"She's leaving?"

"Yes, and I don't want to go alone to take her off the island."

Emily glanced over her shoulder at the chaotic kitchen. "I'm trying to pack. You know I'm leaving tomorrow."

"As if I could forget."

He waited while she gazed at him then heaved a sigh. "All right, I'll come, but you have to bring me home after. I can't stay for lunch at your house, and I don't want Felicia to see me on shore or she'll find something for me to do."

"Don't you want a chance to interview Pauli?"

"Not really. And she probably doesn't want to talk to me. Her brother was arrested yesterday for two terrible crimes. That's not something a woman is apt to want to talk about."

Nate had his doubts about that. Given the chance, Pauli Derbin would talk, probably at great length, to put her own spin on the recent events.

To his surprise, when they arrived at the isolated cottage, Pauli gave them a subdued welcome. She indicated the bags and boxes she wanted to take with her, and Nate made four trips down to the boat before everything was loaded.

When he at last leaned over to cast off from the dock, he saw that, as he'd anticipated, Pauli was baring her soul to Emily, and Emily was scribbling notes on the back of a flyer advertising Vital Women Wilderness Retreat.

"When I called the attorney from the

marina last night, he told me Andrew has confessed to killing Grandpa and Josh Slate." Pauli's blue eyes were bloodshot, and her mascara clumped in dark smudges beneath her eyes. "I just can't believe it. I thought Andrew loved Grandpa. He's the one who came up here every summer to fish with Grandpa, and he always seemed fond of him."

"Maybe something happened between them," Emily suggested.

Nate hesitated to leave the mooring and start the motor, as their voices were so low. This conversation was important. He rearranged Pauli's luggage, then found a line to fiddle with, uncoiling and recoiling it unnecessarily, and took his time to stow it in a locker.

"I guess it couldn't have been an accident." Pauli pulled a bandanna from her straw tote bag and wiped her tears, smearing the mascara further.

"Do you think Andrew was angry with him?" Emily asked.

"He was certainly upset a few weeks ago. Grandpa told us that he was going to sell the cottage and the rest of the island."

"How did you feel about that?" Emily asked.

Pauli shrugged. "I wasn't happy with it,

but after all, it was Grandpa's choice to make. He's owned this land for over half a century. He'd decided to sell the cottage lots when he needed money, and then he sold that tract to Raven. I figured he could do what he wanted to do with the rest. But Andrew . . ."

"What?" Emily asked softly.

"He was frantic." Pauli stared at Emily. "I should have realized. He was upset all out of proportion to what was happening. Of course, I never dreamed he had something to hide. I thought he just wanted to keep the cottage."

Nate sat down a few feet away from them to wait for Pauli to finish her tale. He imagined Andrew's panic when the thought of someone exploring the hilltop and finding Josh's last resting place loomed before him.

"He told me he was going to come up here and talk to Grandpa about his wanting to sell. Andrew even said something about offering to buy it himself if he could get financing."

"When was that?" Emily asked.

Pauli's eyes lost their focus. "Hmm . . . about three weeks ago, I guess. Then I got a call saying Grandpa was dead. Of course I called Andrew immediately to see if they'd notified him. And I asked him if he'd been up to talk to Grandpa, but he said he hadn't. He'd been busy, and there wasn't time."

"But you know now that he did," Emily said.

Pauli nodded. "How could he do that? I mean, it was *Grandpa!* And all this week, Andrew's been consoling me and saying how terrible it was that someone did that."

"I'm so sorry, Pauli." Emily set aside her pen and paper and leaned over to embrace her. Nate was amazed to see the haughty young woman collapse into Emily's arms and weep.

At last Pauli straightened and sniffed, applying the soggy bandanna to her tear-streaked face. "I guess he thought that if the land stayed in the family, no one would ever find the grave. But then he went and told Raven he might sell it to her. That made me so mad! Was he going to tell her Josh was buried up there?"

"I don't know," Emily said.

"Well, I talked to Raven this morning, and I believe her story. She says she never knew where Josh's body was."

Emily nodded. "I believe her, too. Nate and I were with her when she told the police what happened, and she was determined to tell them everything she knew."

"But Josh . . ." Pauli inhaled deeply and looked up, beyond the cottage to the forested hillside behind it. "I wanted to think Andrew and Rocky were just stupid and didn't want to report that Josh was dead and get all the kids at the party in trouble, so they buried him. But the police say it was more than that."

Emily squeezed Pauli's hand. "It's hard to accept, isn't it?"

Fresh tears spilled down Pauli's cheeks. "Until I hear him say it under oath, I won't believe it. That he killed Josh, too, I mean."

Nate pressed his lips together. He didn't like that image, either. The jealous teenager, finding his rival unconscious on the beach, deciding in a split second to finish him off. How was Raven feeling about that now?

Emily held a fresh tissue out to Pauli. "Go home and get some rest. Give yourself some time. When they allow it, go and see your brother."

"Are you going to publish all this?" Pauli stiffened suddenly, eyeing Emily as she might a leech.

"Not if you don't want me to."

Pauli's lips twitched. "I guess . . . well, they'll announce that he confessed, won't they? Andrew's lawyer said something about a press conference."

"We can just go with what the police spokesman releases," Emily said. "Unless you want to say something to people who will read about it."

Pauli sat for a moment, examining her hands. She nudged one fingernail with her thumbnail, where the polish had chipped. "There is something I'd like to say to the people of Baxter."

Emily reached for her paper. "Felicia will publish anything within reason, Pauli."

"Thank you. I'd like to apologize to my hometown. I'm devastated by this, and I know the people here are having as much trouble understanding it as I am. I wish I could change things for Josh Slate's family, and for all the kids who were at that party, and for everyone who knew my grandpa and loved him." Her tears flowed freely. "And I would like to announce that when all of this is over, I intend to sell the rest of Grand Cat Island to Raven Miller for her retreat center."

Nate blinked and stared at Pauli. For the first time, he spoke up. "Is Raven still planning to expand Vital Women? I'd heard she was making other plans."

"She is." Pauli managed a watery smile. "She told me she wants to close Vital

Women and change the center into a Christian family retreat. She even has a name for it already. Surpassing Peace Retreat Center."

"That's wonderful," Emily said.

Nate nodded. "Terrific."

"She wants to close for the rest of the summer and reopen next spring," Pauli said. "I told her that as soon as Grandpa's estate is settled, I'll sell to her. And I hope to be one of her first guests. I could use a little of that surpassing peace she seems to have found."

22

Emily fit the image of the typical Baxter resident in late July. Sunglasses, shorts, T-shirt, sandals. But Nate spotted her the instant she stepped through the doorway of the marina. She'd had her hair trimmed, and it barely brushed her shoulders. Pulling her glasses off, she blinked, searching the aisles.

She'd been away three weeks. Nothing had changed. Everything had changed.

His heart pounded as he shoved the last bottle of Moxie into the cooler and strode toward her. Her blue eyes focused on him, and she grinned, extending her arms to him. He folded her against his chest, easing her away from the door, into a niche between the postcard rack and the maple sugar display.

"Welcome home," he whispered in her ear and stooped to kiss her, thankful and relieved. She'd made the long drive alone safely, and he hoped she'd never be away so long again.

Emily clung to him for a moment then stepped back. "Are you ready for a ton of loading? I had to rent a trailer. Didn't know I had so much stuff."

"I've got the two oldest Kimmel boys waiting out back. We can use two boats. That way, we should have you all moved in an hour."

"Great." She stood on tiptoe and kissed his cheek. "Mom's coming up next weekend for a visit. I want to have it all nice by then."

She was right. It was a lot of stuff, but that was okay. It meant she was here to stay. Two hours later he paid the two boys off at Emily's new dock. She stood beside him, waving and watching them take their small motorboat down the shore to their parents' cottage.

"So, this place is officially yours now?" They turned and walked slowly along the dock toward shore, and he slid his arm around her waist.

"Uh-huh. I insisted that Mom accept what was fair market value, but she still gave me a very good price. I made the down payment yesterday."

He squeezed her against his side as they stepped onto the pine-needle-strewn path.

"Em, I'm so glad you're staying."

She grinned up at him. "Well, I'm taking a big cut in salary, but Felicia's sure she can pay me enough to cover groceries and installments on the cottage."

"What will you do in the fall?"

"I think I can find a place to room on shore over the winter. Then, when the ice goes out, I'll come back out here."

"Perfect."

As they went up the path, Nate was happier than he'd ever been before. The shadows of the pines were friendly now, and the disturbing memories put to rest.

"There is something I need to talk to you about," he said as they approached the steps.

"Something we haven't covered by phone in the last three weeks? I thought we'd hit every possible topic."

"Well, this is a little surprise, you might say." He looked down into her eyes. "My mom and Pastor Phillips are getting married."

"That's not a surprise. I saw it coming a month ago."

"Yeah, well . . . it puts some other things in motion."

Emily studied him and nodded. "Come on in. I put coffee on while you and the boys were getting those last boxes."

He settled at the pine table, trying to plan his announcement. She poured their mugs full and sat across from him.

"Okay. Tell me the real news."

He looked down at his mug, picked it up, and set it back on the table.

"Em, I've decided I still want to be a cop. Being around Gary and the others while they worked on the murders . . . well, I've always wanted to go into criminal justice. You know that."

She smiled, just a little at first, then broader and broader, until her whole face was filled with joy.

"Wonderful."

"You really think so?"

"Yes, but who will run the marina?"

He took a sip of coffee then faced her again. "Mom and I are talking about . . . about selling it."

Emily was silent for several seconds. "Wow."

"Yeah."

"You're right. I wasn't ready for that."

Nate shifted in his chair. He'd outlined his presentation in his mind, but now all order had fled. "We're just thinking about it. They want to get married in the fall, and Mom will keep her job as postmistress until then. But . . . well, I'll have to go away for a while."

Emily nodded. "Selling the business would help pay for it. How long will it take you to finish your degree?"

He gulped and reached for the sugar bowl.

"Nate, you drink your coffee black."

He set the sugar bowl down and leaned back in the chair. "I'm not going to finish my degree. Em, I went to Bangor yesterday and put in an application with the county sheriff's department."

"You . . . what?"

"I talked to Gary for a long time. I had thought I'd apply with the state police, but they could send me anywhere. I want to stay here. Baxter's too small for its own police department, and Aswontee isn't hiring right now, but —"

"Wait, wait!" She held up her hands, and he stopped talking. "They can hire you, just like that?"

"Well, yeah. I talked to the county sheriff yesterday, and he was encouraging. He said I'd make a good candidate, and with the education I have, they could hire me and send me to the Maine Criminal Justice Academy for training."

"The police academy? That's in Waterville."

"Vassalboro. I know. It's about two hours from here."

Her face was a blank.

This isn't going well. Lord, show me what to say to her, if You want me to do this.

He reached for her hands and held them gently on the table. "Look, I've had this . . . this interest, I guess you could say . . . this desire . . . since I was a kid, but I decided back when Dad died that God didn't want me to pursue it. I mean, Mom needed me here, and . . ."

Emily's eyes glistened with tears. "I understand."

"You do?" He squeezed her hands.

"Yeah. Things are different now."

He nodded. "A lot different. I never expected to have the chance again, you know? But every time I talked to Gary this month, it seemed more and more feasible. I started praying about it, and . . . I wanted to talk to you first, but yesterday it all seemed to come together, so I put in the application. Are you mad, Em?"

She squeezed his hands so tightly it hurt. "No. I'm happy for you."

Joy spurted up in Nate's heart as he gazed at her. "I should have told you. But I wanted to wait until you came back and . . . tell you in person."

"You did. You are."

They both laughed.

"So . . . you're not upset?"

"No. I've always thought you'd be a terrific cop. You've got the brain for investigative work."

He sat without moving and let that sink in. "Thanks. Of course, I'd have to do a lot of other stuff first, not all of it pleasant."

She relaxed her grip just a bit. "It might be kind of dangerous."

He shrugged. "I dealt with that a long time ago. Gary says being a cop in Maine is less dangerous than bungee jumping."

"Now, that I believe." Emily's smile was a bit crooked.

"Any job has risks, and to me, it's worth it."

She nodded soberly. "All right, but when all the reporters start hounding you for stories about the crimes you're investigating . . ."

"What, babe?"

"You have to brief the *Journal* first."

"Well, I don't know. That might be a conflict of interest."

She stood, and Nate jumped up to meet her at the end of the table. She tumbled into his arms, and he held her, warm and pliant, against him.

"The only bad thing I can see is, you're just coming back," he whispered. "I don't want to leave now!"

"We'll get through it. The training is less than a year, right?"

"Oh, yeah. Four months or so. And I'd come home weekends. That's if they hire me. They haven't said for sure yet. But we've got Allison full time now at the marina, and I've interviewed a couple of guys interested in handling the boats. Jobs are scarce. I don't think we'll have a problem getting help until we decide if we want to sell."

She smiled up at him. "Sounds like you've thought it through."

"I have. And I wasn't trying to keep it from you."

"I know. It'll be good, Nate. For both of us."

"You think so?"

"Yes. I mean, if we love each other . . ."

"What do you mean, if?" He pushed away and squinted down at her. "That's not at question, is it?"

She snuggled in against his chest with a sigh. "No, it's definite. I love you. There's never been anyone but you, Nate. Whether you're running the marina or chasing criminals, I love you."

He bent to kiss her, relishing a mingled contentment and sweet anticipation. Emily was home to stay.

ABOUT THE AUTHORS

Susan Page Davis is the author of seven historical novels, two children's novels, and three romantic suspense books, in addition to cozy mysteries. She and her husband, Jim, live in beautiful Maine, where he is a news editor. Both are active in a small, independent Baptist church. Their six children range in age from 13 to 30, and when possible they enjoy spending time with their five grandchildren. Susan has homeschooled all six children, and the youngest two are still learning at home. She enjoys reading, needlework, genealogy, and meeting her readers. Coauthoring the MAINEly Murder mystery series with her daughter is one of the many blessings brought into her life through writing fiction. Visit her Web site at: www.susanpage davis.com

Megan Elaine Davis grew up in rural

Maine where she was homeschooled with her five siblings. She holds a bachelor of arts degree in creative writing from Bob Jones University, and has published poetry, articles, and humorous anecdotes in various publications. Besides writing, she enjoys reading, travel, theater, cooking, and chatting with friends. Her favorite authors are Agatha Christie, Jane Austen, and C. S. Lewis. *Homicide at Blue Heron Lake* is her first novel. She lives in Clinton, Maine.